Echoes in The Darkness

The Darkbound Saga

Book 2 of 5

By Grayson Sharp

Echoes in The Darkness

Book Two of the Darkbound Saga

© 2025 Grayson Sharp
Published by Darkbound Publishing

ISBN (Paperback): 979-8-9999396-2-3
ISBN (Hardcover): 979-8-9999396-3-0

Cover design by Grayson Sharp with Canva AI.
Printed in the United States of America

This is a work of fiction. Names, characters, places, and incidents are products of the author's imagination or are used fictitiously. Any resemblance to actual events, locales, or persons, living or dead, is entirely coincidental.

First Edition

Trigger Warning

Violence & Gore

Death & loss

Abduction & imprisonment

Psychological trauma

Suicidal ideation

Substance use

Strong language

Cartel/organized crime themes

Torture & abuse

Sexual references (non-graphic)

Weapons & warfare

Inspirational Playlist

Throttle Therapy – Ruby Darkrose

Life Support – Citizen Soldier

Bullet Proof – Citizen Soldier

Figure Me Out – Citizen Soldier

Indestructible – Disturbed

Are You Ready – Disturbed

Feel Invincible – Skillet

Judgment Day – Five Finger Death Punch

Another Chance – SON BROKU & 52Blu

The Legend Never Dies – SON BROKU & 52Blu

Courtesy Call – Thousand Foot Krutch

Decisions – Big Ro6

Table of Contents

Prologue

Oh, hey you're back. I'm guessing you're wanting some answers huh? Yeah, well get in line cause I want some too. This is bullshit!!! There was at least half a dozen men, if not more that came barging in. Took out 3 before they got me. Yeah, Jace I know, it's not my fault. Say that all you want but- Oh shut the fuck up Lucian, like you could do better? Mister *only here for the sex*. It's not like you have any hidden skill set that would have been useful.

Like I was saying, it was six to one. I did what I could but they still...they still...still...

What Michael is trying to say is that they still took her. We are going to be getting her back. One way or another, we will find her. I just hope we are not too late.

You all need to shut the fuck up! Michael you're fucking useless. I could have taken them if I wasn't being held back. He's still got me locked up. Why the fuck can't I get out. I hate being caged. I will break this god damn mind and body if you don't let me go. I swear to fucking god-

ENOUGH!

The Plan

Michael

"Michael...Jace...Lucian....are one of you awake in there?"

I hear our names being called. But it sounds like the person is under water. Damn, why does my head hurt so damn much? I wasn't drinking last night, right? No wait, it's coming back. Madison, last night, then this morning, the cartel, Marco. God the more I think, harder this headache hits.

"Hey you awake? I see your eyes moving, come on man talk to me, open your eyes."

I do just that, opening my eyes I come face to face with the last person I expected to see. "Jack, what the hell are you doing here?" I say pinching the bridge of my nose.

"I saw that man leave last night after I watched him follow you and Madison back to your place." he says with a worried look on his face.

The pounding in my head eases a little as I process his words. Scanning his face, I can tell something's wrong.

Lucian is the first to speak up, *he's hiding something.*

Or he's scared out of his mind. Look at his hands Michael. Jace interrupts.

Yeah I can see his hands and it's obvious he's hiding something. I've gotta play this safe though.

"You mean the guy that was too scared to take the shot when it was just Mads and I in the elevator? And you haven't answered my question, what the hell are you doing here?"

He gets up off the ground and starts pacing. Rubbing his hands together and then on his jeans. He starts to twiddle his thumbs.

"Jack, what the fuck is going on and how the hell did you know to come check on me? Your bar is half a mile away, and you don't like leaving it."

"Ok ok" he says finally. "I ended up following that guy last night after he left. I thought I was keeping enough space and distance to stay undetected like you taught me." He pauses for moment.

"And...?"

"And I guess I still need work." he says as his face drops. "They threatened to kill my Amelia if I didn't cooperate. I didn't have choice man."

My hands ball up tight. My heart rate picks up. This fucking bastard sold Madison and I out. The edges of my vison start to blur. But where I would normally feel HIM clawing up from the depths, eager to take over, there's only silence. No weight pressing at the back of my skull. No shadow grinning behind my eyes. The absence is louder than his screams, and it makes my skin crawl. Where the hell is he?

I turn my full attention back to Jack. Getting up and grabbing him by his shirt I slam him against the closest wall, "So instead of-"

Don't even go there Michael, you can't fault him for wanting to protect his little girl, Jace says.

Were you really going to blame Jack like that? Come on Michael, you're better than this, Lucian follows up.

I take a step back, releasing him. What the fuck have I gotten myself into? Just a few weeks ago I was coming in from a three-month job. Just trying to get a little rest and now I have this mystery woman that comes seeking me out but not really seeking ME out. More like the other guy. That's another thing, how the hell did she know about HIM? How the hell did she know about us?

I sit down at my desk, leaning forward I rub my hands down my face and try to calm down.

We need answers, I tell the others.

Yeah, no shit sherlock, now get to asking, Lucian snaps back.

Let's try and remain calm, Jace interjects, ever the voice of reason, right?

Screw that, Lucian says, *cuffs are in second drawer, don't let Jack go just yet. I have a feeling he is going to get really talkative pretty soon.* For once I agree with the psycho.

Almost as if he could hear the convo I was having with the others, Jack starts heading towards the front door. I lunge forward grab him by the back of his neck and throw him in the chair I was just in.

After getting the cuffs and a few of the restraints on him, I go to the kitchen and make a pot a coffee. I need my wits about me, plus Jace won't shut the hell up. You'd think he was made of the stuff with how much he drinks it. I down the first mug and poor another.

Heading back into my room, I see Jack trying to free himself. He takes one look at me and freezes.

"Jackie boy, Jackie boy.... you care to tell me what you know? Or am I going to have to take some extreme measures?"

"Listen" he says, "they threatened to kill Ameilia, and you know I would do anything for her."

I stay quiet, just staring with that predator's gaze. All men eventually talk. It's just a matter of knowing your prey and knowing when to stalk and when to pounce.

"Like I said" he starts, see told you, "I was tailing the guy after he left you and Madison. Followed him for a while, when out of nowhere he turns smiles and then winks at me. Yeah, you heard me right, winks. Then I'm hit over the head and thrown in this old rusty Oldsmobile."

I continue to stare at the poor excuse of a man in front of me. Scanning him for any lies or deceit. So far, he is on point, "Continue" I say, as I head over to my bed to sit.

"Well, we drove for a while and I also had a bag over my head, so I don't know where they took me, but I do remember it smelled like one of those old dog food factories." he says

"Get to the details about how the fuck you knew to come check on me."

"Yeah ok. So, I'm brought to some guy they called 'El jefe' and he said that he's going to give you a little visit because you have something that belongs to him. I tried to tell him that you had just gotten back not too long ago from a three-month job, but he wasn't having it."

Sounds believable, Jace says.

We need more, keep the pressure on him, Lucian demands

Listen I know what the fuck I'm doing here. It's not like any of you really go on those 'jobs' I go to, I snap. *You know, the ones that give us the freedom to do whatever the fuck you want.*

Silence is all I hear from them.

"Did he happen to mention this 'something' I had? What it looked like? Was it small or big? Square or round? Anything helps really."

"Will you please uncuff me? I'm not going to run. Hell, I came here to check on you." he says

"Yeah, but you knew all night and didn't even bother with a text. That shows me that he made you talk and that you made a deal. Obviously for Amelia's sake and I applaud you for that. You're a great father Jack."

"No, I swear I didn't do anything like that. He just held me hostage all night. I didn't see Amelia or anyone else till around four or five this morning. I grabbed her and we ran as fast as we could, I eventually got a cab. I swear man, that's it. I'm just checking on someone I thought was my friend." Jack says with tears streaming down his face. I hate it when they cry.

I pull the knife from the drawer in my nightstand. Slowly walking over to Jack I can see the terror in his eyes. The same terror I've seen countless times before. When grown men twice my size realize that the monster they thought they were is nothing compared to me. Some shit themselves, vomit, and yeah, they piss themselves also. And I'll never get tired of seeing that look on their face. How the air around them changes to bitter sweetness, right before their life ends. How after I plunge my blade deep in their chest, I hear their staggering breath. It's like music to my ears. My heart soars, and HIM finally calms down.

Michael, he's our friend. Jace begins to beg, *we've had dinner with him, drank at his bar, shared stories. Don't do this, there has to be another way.*

He's the reason Madison is gone. He led them right to us. He's the reason they took her from us, from ME!

Lucian's voice is low, steady, commanding. *As much as I agree with you Michael, Jack was only doing what he thought was best to save his little girl. Put the knife away.*

Enough out of you two. I'm done listening, it's time to act. Time to do what I do best.

I'm fast, real fast. Fast enough that Jack jumps when my hand shoots out and grabs the back of his neck. I draw my arm back, blade in hand ready to strike and that's when I stop. My fingers moving over a bump on the back of his neck.

"You get a new tattoo Jack?" my eyes still starring straight into his.

"N-no....w-why?" he says, snot and tears covering his face.

I pull his head down and he screams. "Shut the fuck up, I just want to check something."

I see a small little cut right at the base of his neck. I take my knife and very quickly re-open the already fresh scar.

Jack kicks and screams some more as I take a pair of needle nose I had on my desk and pull out a small little device.

"Will you shut the fuck up my guy. Look!"

Jack stops long enough to look up and I take his shirt and wipe his face off.

W-was that in me?" he asks

"Yeah....Jack? Do you recall how long you were there? Did you at some point go to sleep?"

"Well, not intentionally. They fed me, and then about an hour later I was out" he says "but I'm serious, I wasn't trying to sleep, I was too worried about Amelia. I needed to get to her."

"You didn't stop to think that maybe it was just a little off that the people who kidnapped your daughter and you, would offer to feed you? Are you really this fucking dense Jack?"

"Well, what do you think happened?" He says with a look I could only describe as total idiocy.

Jace pipes up really quick. *Be nice, you have to remember that not everyone thinks like you Michael. Jack sounds completely innocent. Right Lucian?*

Nothing for a beat and then, *Yeah, I got to agree with the boy scout. As messed up as the situation is, Jack sounds like he's telling the truth.*

Fine, I say with a roughness to my voice that lets the others know I'm getting close to losing it. Hell, I kind of did a moment ago.

I can take the wheel for a while. It's no biggie. Jace ask more like a question than a statement.

It's fine, I say *besides, where we are going, I'm the one that's going to need to be behind the wheel.* I say staring at the little electronic in my hands.

I can feel their gazes on me. They know I'm talking about Z. I don't care what anyone says that crazy purple haired hacker is the best in the world. And if we are going to get to the bottom of where they took Madison, there's no one better to have at your side than Z.

"Alright Jack, you're clear. Let me get you out of those cuffs and restraints. Sorry about this, I just had to be sure you know."

"I understand that, but can I ask you a question?" he says

"You just did Jack." I say with a ghost of laugh behind it.

"You're extremely fast, and stronger than most people I know. Your skills with a blade are pretty lethal and scary. So, what is it you really do for work? And don't give me that subcontractor bs" he says with an annoyed look on his face.

"Thats a story for another time, Jackie boy. Let's get some coffee in you and I'll look at your wrist really quick."

He looks away rubbing his wrist "No that's fine, it doesn't hurt."

"Listen I'm sorry, but I had to be certain that you didn't flip on me. Now let me see your wrist and I can bandage you up."

He holds out his hands. They aren't that bad. They'll be healed in a few days.

"Hey, you said you rushed over here with Amelia, where is she?" I say as I'm wrapping his wrist.

Thats when I hear the faint cooing of a newborn.

She's been here the whole fucking time? Holy fuck!

You about ended that kids only living parent not even ten feet away from her! Jace screams at me,

Talk about the start of another Dexter tv show huh? Huh? Oh, come one, you guys have no sense of humor. Lucian adds.

"She's in the living room on the couch. I'm surprised you didn't see her when you walked out there earlier." he says.

"Well, I was a little preoccupied if you remember correctly, and also she must be a really good kid to stay quiet while her dad was being interrogated not even ten feet away."

He smiles and chuckles, and then starts laughing, which makes me laugh, breaking the tension finally.

"Yeah, she's a good kid that's for sure." he says after he calms himself down.

"Well Jack, I'm off to see an old friend. Feel free to stay a while if you want. I've got coffee in the pot, and there's food in fridge. Make yourself at home. Just lock up when you leave."

"Will do.... oh, Michael before you go. I was able to figure out where they were going to go after they got whatever it was, they came to get from you." he says.

A beat passes and then, "Well spit it the fuck out man. Where are they headed to?"

"I found a flight path for a plane that's supposed to leave later tonight but I could only make out the town before they moved me. Have you heard of a town called Barceloneta?"

What the fuck? Why? Of all the places in the world, why the fuck is he making me chase her to Puerto Rico?

Throttle Therapy

After grabbing a quick shower and packing a bag. I say my goodbyes to Jack, grab my coat and hit the streets. It's cold as fuck right now here in New York. The kind of cold that bites straight through leather and into bone. But that's fine, I need the bite. I need the pain.

The city hums like a restless beast, but all I hear is the blood pounding in my ears. HIM should be stirring, clawing to take the wheel, but the silence is still there. Its deafening. That absence sits heavier than the winter air pressing against my lungs. If I can't drown it out in here, ill drown it out on the road.

I make it to the storage a few blocks away in no time. Punching in the gate code, I catch movement out the corner of my eye. An Oldsmobile creeping past on the street. Not just any olds either, the kind too clean to be that old, likes it's been babied for a reason. My gut knots. They're still here, watching, waiting.

They're still here. They must have had someone watching. I say

We can't fight right now, Jace says, *as much as I dislike Z, we actually do need her help to find Madison.*

Exactly what I was thinking, Lucian chimes in, *and you only don't like Z because she shot you down when we first met her in London.*

Now's not the time to rehash old wounds fellas, be quiet and let me think.

I don't flinch. Don't look twice. Just let the gate grind open and walk inside like I don't have a care in the world. If I react they win. So I keep my head down, hands stuffed in my coat pockets, playing the role of a man too tired to notice anything but the cold.

The cameras on the corners pick me up as I pass row after row of storage units, boots crunching in the thin layer of salt scattered across the pavement. I can feel their eyes on my back, but I force myself not to hurry. Not yet. Let them think I'm just here to grab some junk, maybe a box of old clothes. Nothing worth following me in for.

Only when the metal door of unit 17 is in front of me do I let the mask slip, just a fraction. My hands twitch with the need to tear that Olds apart, piece by piece. But I've got other plans tonight. I need the bike, I need the ride, I need the speed. And I need to get to Z.

I slide the key into the padlock and twist, the metal clicking louder than it should in the quiet winter. Rolling the door up, the smell hits first—oil, rubber, gasoline. My kind of incense. Home.

And there she is. Matte black, all sharp angles and coiled muscle. Chrome catching what little light there is, glinting like a blade. Built for speed, not comfort. A predator crouched on two wheels, waiting to be unleashed. My bike. My therapy. The only thing that's never let me down.

I run a hand over the fairings, the plastic smooth and cold beneath my palm. Every line of her frame screams velocity. Not meant for long rides, not meant for lazy cruising, she's meant to cut through the city like a bullet. Bag slung over my shoulder, I wheel her onto the pavement and swing a leg over. Key in, twist, choke open. The engine growls to life, deep and guttural, echoing off the concrete like a promise. My pulse finally matches the rhythm.
I grip the bars tighter, lean forward, and let the roar settle into my chest. "I'm coming, Mads," I whisper under my breath. "Just need to grab an old friend first."

I roll her out onto the street, tires hissing on the salt crusted pavement. The Oldsmobile is still there, parked just far enough down the block to play it casual. I start to move, one block then two. I can feel them settling into the rhythm on my tail. That's when I crack the throttle and she comes to life. I scream down the avenue, the engines roar bouncing off the glass towers around us. I dart left down a narrow street lined with stacked trash bags and parked cars hugging tight. My bars clear with inches to spare. Their Oldsmobile doesn't. I hear the grind of metal on metal behind me, the scrape of their side panel kissing the parked car. Good.

I let the throttle breathe, the engine purring steady under me. Morning wind cuts my face raw, but I welcome it. As I pull up to a stop a few blocks away, I get this eerie feeling creeping up my neck. I start scanning every intersection, alley, doorway, anything. That's when I spot them, two other riders. Friend or foe, I wonder. I decide to test out my question. Pulling up to a stop light I put on my blinker, they follow suit. Could be coincidence, right?

Not my luck. They turn when I turn, slow when I slow. I pull over and get off the bike. Parking her in front of an old bakery. The smell of fresh baked goods fills the air around me. The Fortunato Brothers Bakery. I remember Jace sneaking away from the foster home countless mornings to come try and get a little of their famous cannoli's. Sweet ricotta, crisp shell, sugar on my fingers before the sun was even up. For a kid with nothing, the taste was the only good thing the city ever gave me. A buck fifty bought me ten minutes of peace. Worth every damn penny.

Cute story, Lucian mutters, voice sharp in the back of my skull. *But maybe save the trip down memory lane for when you're not being tailed, huh?*

Jace cuts in softer but firm. *He's right, Michael. Those two riders haven't taken their eyes off you since you stopped. Either call them out or move. Standing still isn't helping.*

I blink, shake off the sugar and warmth of the memory. They're right. The past is gone. Right now, it's just me and the bike, and whoever the hell thinks they can box me in at dawn.

Enough nostalgia. I kick the stand back, rev the throttle, and the bike roars against the morning quiet. The two shadows behind me rev in answer. Game on.

I thread through a line of cabs stacked at a red light, horns blaring as I split the lane. The riders follow, but they're slower, cautious. A box truck lumbers into the intersection just as I clear it. One of them doesn't. Brakes scream, rubber burns. One down. One to go.

Two blocks down, I cut left without signaling, slipping between a garbage truck and a delivery van unloading bread. Mirrors scrape my shoulders, but the bike slices through like a blade. In my mirror, the rider hesitates. I gun it, leaning hard into the next corner, tires screaming against the pavement. The rider commits, chasing too close, too desperate. A yellow cab cuts across the lane and I slip by clean, but he isn't so lucky. Metal shrieks, glass shatters, and in my mirror I catch the bike cartwheeling across the asphalt. No more headlights. No more tail. Just me and the road.

I lean into the throttle, the bike answers like she's been waiting all morning to breathe. The scream of the engine tears through the morning quiet, echoing off glass towers and steel bridges. The cold stings my face, needles in the air, but I welcome it. It keeps me sharp. Keeps me awake.

The city blurs past in streaks of gray and gold. Steam rises from manhole covers like ghosts escaping, curling around the bike as I slice through. The streets aren't empty, not in New York, but they're thin. Delivery trucks crawl, cabs prowl, the occasional straggler stumbles home from last night's bad decisions. All background noise. The only thing I hear is the bike beneath me and the blood pounding in my ears.

Better, Jace murmurs, always the calm one. *Focus, keep your head on the road.*

Lucian laughs, sharp and bitter. *He's not focusing. He's trying to drown us out. HIM should be here by now, and he's not. You feel it, don't you, Michael? That silence chewing at our ribs?*

I twist the throttle harder, engine snarling as the world tilts and pulls. HIM isn't here, and for once, I don't care. The bike is enough.

I rocket down Broadway, the early sun bleeding against the horizon, painting the asphalt in fire. A garbage truck heaves into the intersection, its brakes squealing like a wounded animal. I cut hard, dipping low, my knee almost grazing the pavement as I slip past. Horns blare. A driver spits curses out his window, but I'm gone before the words catch up.

A delivery truck door slams open, men unloading bread racks to corner store. For a moment, the smell cuts through the exhaust, but it doesn't take me back, it only reminds me how long it's been since I had the luxury of stopping for something simple. Peace isn't on the menu anymore.

You're slipping again, Lucian cuts in. *Living in the past won't save Madison.*

I'm not slipping, I mutter, leaning forward, letting the bike eat the road. *I'm burning it out.*

Throttle. Breath. Heartbeat.

The rhythm pounds into me like a war drum. Every ghost, every job, every man I've put in the ground, they all claw at the back of my skull, screaming to be remembered. But here, on this machine, at this speed, they can't touch me.

The Williamsburg Bridge rises ahead, a steel skeleton stretching across the river. I gun it, the bike vibrating under me as the city falls away behind. The East River flashes silver below, waves catching the first light of day like shards of glass. My reflection stares back for half a second before it's gone.

Faster, Lucian urges, almost gleeful. *Push it till the wheels melt.*

Or until you wrap us around a light pole, Jace snaps back.

I ignore them both. The bridge belongs to me. Each lane a vein, each vibration a heartbeat. My heartbeat.

The streets on the other side open up wider, traffic thinning as Brooklyn wakes slowly. Red lights flicker like warnings, but they're nothing but dares to me. I blow through them, tires screaming, wind tearing at my coat. Neon signs buzz weakly against the dawn, half-lit promises of bodegas and corner stores. A jogger freezes at the crosswalk, eyes wide as I slice by close enough for him to feel the wind.

For a second, I imagine what it looks like from the outside—just a blur of matte black and a rider hunched low, head down, nothing but speed and rage holding him together. Maybe that's all I am. A shadow that learned how to bleed.

Throttle therapy, I whisper, the words lost in the roar. Not a cure, but it burns enough to scrub me clean.

I slow only when I turn down a side street. The roar of the bike drops to a growl, echoing between brick walls tagged with graffiti, the kind of art only New York can make.

Z's place doesn't look like much. It never does. Just another brick building with rusted fire escapes and windows covered in blackout curtains. But I know better. The lines are too clean, the locks too new, the wires too carefully hidden. You don't walk into Z's without her knowing you're coming.

I kill the engine. Silence slams into me, heavy and immediate, and I almost miss the roar. My therapy's over. The ghosts creep back in at the edges, waiting to sink their teeth.

Lucian hums low, amused. *Showtime.*

I swing off the bike, grab my bag, and look up at the building. The city breathes around me, cold and unforgiving, but I don't move. Not yet. I let the silence sit, let it settle deep.

Then I whisper, steady and low. *I'm coming, Mads. Just need to wake the devil's favorite little hacker.*

Old Friends

(Michaels pov)

I'm walking into Z's place when my phone beeps.

Z: Its open, come on up.
Me: On my way.

I pocket my phone and make my way up the five flights of stairs. Leave it to a paranoid schizophrenic hacker to live on the top floor. But when you do the kind of work we do, it makes sense after a while. Better to see who's coming, rather than be caught off guard.

The fifth flight of stairs groans under my boots, each step echoing in the narrow stairwell. The walls are cracked paint, old plaster, the kind of building where the rents cheap and neighbors keep their heads down. But when I reach the top, the vibe shifts. The door isn't some flimsy wooden panel with a deadbolt. Its reinforced steel, matte black, the hinges sunk deep. Not something you pick open in under a minute. This is a bunker dressed like an apartment.

I knock once. Nothing. A pause, long enough for me to feel the weight of cameras I can't see. My neck prickles. She's watching.

"You better say the password old man." I hear from the other side.

"Old man? That's new Z"

"I'm not hearing the password." I hear her thick New York accent. Coming from a small little psycho like her, you'd think it's cute. But Z is all that, and then some.

"Sing it old man: Z's the shot you couldn't take. Saved your ass, make no mistake."

"Z's the shot I couldn't take. Saved my ass. No mistake."

The lock clicks with a sound too clean for a building this old. The door opens on its own, slow, deliberate, and I step inside.

"Still hurts, huh? Good. Keeps you honest." I hear Z say.

No sooner do I shut the door and she's already launched herself towards me. I catch her just in time as she wraps her tiny little arms and frame around me in what I assume is her version of a bear hug.

The apartment is nothing like the stairwell. Cold glow from half a dozen monitor's paint the walls in shifting light. Cables snake across the floor like veins, feeding towers of humming servers that throw off a low, steady heat. The air smells of solder, burnt dust, and coffee that's been left on the pot too long. Blackout curtains smother every window, layers thick enough to choke out the dawn outside. For a second, it feels like I stepped out of New York and into another world, one where the only sun rises from LED screens.

She finally releases me and slides down. Z is short, I mean like really short. Just an inch shy of being legally classified as a midget. I think that's why I couldn't take the shot in London.

Z pipes up, a bit of surprise mixed with worry in her voice, "you've got a hell of a way of showing up uninvited."

She drops back into her chair, sighs once, then kicks her boots up on the desk like she owns the whole city. The glow of half a dozen monitors paints her face in shifting blues and greens.

"So, the cartel, huh?" she says, eyes not even on me. Fingers already flying over the keyboard. "You wouldn't be here unless it was bad. And if it's bad enough for you to crawl through five flights of piss-stained stairs, then it's not just bad. It's personal."

I stay quiet, leaning against the wall. The hum of her severs is the only sound between us.

"You want Marco?" she asks flatly. My jaw tightens. She knows. Of course, she knows.

Lucian chuckles in the back of my skull. *Told you. She's always two moves ahead.*

"Don't get cocky, little man," I mutter under my breath. "What was that?" Z asks, smirking without looking. "Nothing."

Her chair creaks as she leans forward, the monitors reflecting in her glasses. "You're lucky I like you, old man. Otherwise, I'd tell you to get the fuck out. This isn't London. I don't owe you shit."

London. There it is. The weight of a trigger I couldn't pull. The blood she spilled in my place.

Jace's voice whispers soft, like it always does when the guilt cuts deep. *She saved us that night. Don't forget it.*

The rapid fire clacking of keys fills the room. Line after line of code, server logs, and encrypted message dumps stream across her monitors. Z's in her element, tearing through firewalls like they're paper. Then she freezes, taps a letter, and leans in. "Got him."

My chest tightens. "Marco's moving product through Puerto Rico. Barceloneta from the looks of it." She swivels to face me fully now, grin fading. "But it's not just drugs anymore. He's chasing something else. Something tied to Madison."

The brooch. I subconsciously touch my bag. She notices, shifting her eyes to my hands. "He's not going to find what he's looking for is he?" Staring at her, more like staring through her, I shake my head back forth. I open my bag, reach in and pull out the brooch.

"What the hell is that thing?" she asks.

"It's a brooch," I say, "and a family heirloom, according to Madison."

"So, this guy kid naps your girl, and runs off with her too Puerto Rico, which might I add, the last time you and I went there, we almost didn't make it back." she says exasperated. "Oh, and while we're on the subject of Madison. Care to explain who the heck this girl is? Why she came into 'your' life? Oh, and let's not forget to ask, since I've been watching you, how the heck does she know about the others?"

Jace speaks up, *Wow, she's scarier than HIM right now.*

Please. HIM at least snarls first. She's going straight for the jugular. Lucian replies.

Now is not a suitable time for jokes. I need to calm her down a bit before she blows a fuse.

Slow and steady, Lucian says *like you're approaching a wild beast. Just shut up you two.*

Hey. Jace says, before I decide to focus my full attention back on Z. "Slow down Z, you're going to spaz out again." I say, trying to calm her down. It doesn't work.

Really? 'you're going to spaz out.' *you really thought that would work.* Jace says.

Lucian pipes up, *Yeah Michael, tell the hacker queen to calm down. Brilliant plan. Want to ask her to smile while you're at it?*

I ignore them.

She stares at me, "Talking to your peanut gallery?" she says with a bit of annoyance in her voice. I'm sure if she could kill with a look, I'd be dead. Multiple times by now, given our history.

"Listen here Old Man, I'm the only one that can tell who is behind the driver's seat in that messed up beautiful head of yours, with just one look at you. Then this little stray comes along and thinks she can just play coy? No sir! I want answers and she's got them so yes, I'll help you find her. I'll even help you take down Marco, because I know you won't stop at just getting Madison back. But you better start talking and I mean now! Otherwise, you can just say bye-bye to this info I have right here." she says, hand hovering over her keyboard.

"Alright," I say, "just don't delete a thing."

She smiles and starts laughing. "You're so easy. Like I would erase precious knowledge? Come on, you know me better than that. Now start talking, old man"

Damn it, she's right. I spend the next hour telling her all about the past couple weeks. From running into Madison, the incident at the bar, the pier, Marco, the cartel, everything. And because we don't like to hide anything from each other, I don't skip over the sex. Wouldn't matter anyways, she would find out one way or another. Plus, she's gay. Hell, to be honest, I learned a thing or two from Z. No, not like that. She's just taught me a few tricks here and there.

"Okay, now that I'm caught up, what brings you to my doorstep aside from needing to get Madison back?" Z says while twirling her pigtails.

I exhale, reach into my bag, and pull out the little device I carved out of Jack's neck. The thing feels heavier than it should. Like holding a live round.

Z tilts her head. Eyes narrowing. "Cute. You brought me a party favor." She picks it up, squinting at it between the glow of her monitors. "Not standard cartel hardware. This is cleaner, sharper. Someone paid real good money for this."

Lucian hums low. *Told you. Cartel scum don't have the brains for tech like that.*

Jace cuts in quieter. *Let her work. You know she's already five steps ahead.*

Z spins in her chair, tossing the device once before slotting it into a drawer cluttered with adapters and cable ends. She pulls out something that looks like a Frankenstein USB rig and plugs it into her tower.

"Alright, lets crack open your mystery bug." Her grin returns, all teeth. "Let's see who's been whispering in Marco's ear."

"Talk to me, sweetheart," she mutters, fingers already dancing across the keyboard.

I lean against the wall, arms crossed, forcing myself to stay patient. But the knot in my chest tightens with every second that passes.

Lucian breaks the silence first. *Let her do her job. She doesn't need you breathing down her neck.*

She saved us in London, Jace added gently. *She'll save us here, too.*

The screens flicker, data compiling into maps, grids, and timestamps. Then Z whistles low. "Damn. This isn't cartel make. This is black market grade. Top shelf."

She swivels in her chair to look at me, waving the device like a prize. "Your boy Marco's not just swinging guns and muscle. He bought himself toys. Expensive ones."

My brow furrows. "Bought? From who?"

Z shrugs. "BlackNet. Shadow auction sites. Take your pick. Point is — it's not custom, not unique. But it's good. Really good." She turns back to the monitors, tapping fast. "This little bastard doesn't just track position. It logs routes, records stops and uploads it all to a secured server on a rolling timer. Marco's basically got a breadcrumb trail on anyone he tags."

My fists clench. "So, Jack was a walking beacon."

"Mm-hmm." Z doesn't look back, too locked in. "And guess who that beacon led straight to?"

Her screen lights up with a map — jagged red lines crawling across it like veins. A blinking marker stops at my neighborhood.

My building. The air in my chest freezes.

Lucian chuckles darkly. *Told you, Michael. We never had a chance the moment he planted it.*
Jace's voice is quieter, guiltier. *Jack didn't even know… he was just a pawn.*

Z cuts in, leaning back in her chair with a grin that doesn't quite reach her eyes. "Good news? I can mirror the signal now. Wherever Marco sends his data, I can see it too. So, if Madison's tagged, we'll know."

"And the bad news?" I ask.

"The server it uploads to? Encrypted up the ass. I'll need time to break in. Hours. Maybe a day." She spins back to face me, eyes gleaming. "But once I do… we'll have Marco's entire playbook."

I stare at the blinking red marker burning on the screen, then close my fists until my knuckles ache. "Then crack it, Z. We don't have time."

The glow of monitors fades into dawn creeping through the blackout curtains. My head feels like it's been rattling in an engine block all night. Z hasn't moved except to swap out mugs of coffee, her fingers still flicking across the keyboard like a machine possessed.

Then — a knock. Three light taps on the steel door.

Z doesn't even look up. "It's open, babe."

The door hisses open and in walks a woman carrying a paper bag in one hand and a cardboard coffee tray in the other. She's tall, sharp cheekbones softened by a sleepy smile, a leather jacket half-zipped against the cold.

"Morning, trouble," she says, dropping the bag on the cluttered desk. "And before you fry another circuit in here, I brought bagels."

Jace pipes up immediately, voice warm. *See? Actual food. Civilized people eat this, Michael.*

Lucian sneers. *Bagels? Please. She should've brought whiskey.*

I lean back, watching as Z practically lights up — all the sharp hacker edges softening in an instant. She hops off her chair, plants a quick kiss on her girlfriend's cheek, and snatches the bag like it's treasure.

"You're a lifesaver." Her girl glances at me then, eyebrow raised. "This him?"

Z nods, already tearing into a bagel like she hasn't eaten in days. "Yep. Old man needed a miracle. Thought I'd lend him mine."

"Lucky you," she says, sliding one of the coffees across the table toward me. "Don't get used to it."

The smell of fresh bagels cuts through the recycled air and burnt solder. For one second, it almost feels normal. Almost.

Z drops back into her chair, mouth full, pointing at the monitors with half a bagel. "Server's fighting me, but I cracked a partial log before my better half walked in. Flight plans. Cargo shipments. Puerto Rico's lit up like a Christmas tree."

The girlfriend rolls her eyes, sipping her coffee. "Always the romantic."

Lucian chuckles darkly. *Romance, huh? Only romance I see is her dating her damn keyboard.*

Jace sighs. *Shut up, Lucian. Let them have this.*

I wrap my hands around the coffee, the heat bleeding into my fingers. For the first time in days, I let myself breathe.

Then Z spins her chair around, grin sharp again.

"Eat up, old man. Once I break the rest of this log, we are booking a ticket to Barceloneta."

"We?"

Never Really Free

Madison

The smell of roasted beans and cinnamon rolls lingers in my head, so sharp I almost believe I'm back there. The chatter of the coffee shop, the steam curling from Jace's mug as he leaned across the table with that stupid grin.

"So," he said, eyes teasing but curious, "do I get to call you mystery woman...or is there a name that comes with all this frostbite?"

For a second, I let myself sit in that memory. Safe. Warm. Seen. I'm jerked back to reality as we hit another rock on the dirt road that leads to Marcos's compound.

It's been almost forty-eight hours since I was taken. In that time, I've been drugged, beaten, tortured. You think of it, I've experienced it. All for a damn brooch that's rightfully mine. Damn my nana for selling that damn thing. Although, I guess if she hadn't, my mother wouldn't still be here.

Come on guys, I need you right now. Where's those smarts at Michael, huh? Jace, I know you have the courage to do what's right, and I need that now. Hell, even you Lucian, mister pretty boy. But as I think of them, the one I really want, the one I went in search of, off of just a rumor. The one that will tear this world apart for me comes to mind, HIM.

I didn't expect to fall so hard for all of them. I tried to keep the distance. Tried to draw HIM out after I'd finally seen the truth. And man was it shocking.

(Weeks Earlier)

The bar was loud, bodies pressed close, the air thick with whiskey and smoke. I hated it the second I stepped in, but I didn't have anywhere else to go. My fingers brushed the brooch in my pocket, the one Marco would kill me for if he caught me again.

I'd heard the rumors — a man who wasn't just one man. A fighter, a monster, depending on who you asked. Some said he'd saved them. Others said he'd left nothing behind but blood. I didn't even know what he looked like, just a vague description, and a name, a few actually.

That's when I saw him.

Slouched at the bar, a drink in his hand, but not lost in it like the others. His eyes were sharp, too sharp. Not the eyes of a drunk. It was like someone else was steering, buried deep under the alcohol.

I swallowed, my throat dry, and forced my legs to move. If I was wrong, I was walking straight into my grave.

The space beside him opened up like it was waiting for me. I slid onto the stool, my pulse hammering so loud I was sure he could hear it. He turned, slow, deliberate, and for the first time I saw those blue eyes up close.

They weren't empty, they were crowded.

"So." he said, voice low and measured, "what do I call a lady that's bold enough to come sit next to a guy like me?"

The line was casual, maybe even playful, but underneath it I felt the weight of something else, testing me, measuring me. I smirked like I had all the control in the world, even though my hands were trembling in my lap.

"Depends," *I said.* "You good at remembering names?"

His mouth twitched, almost a smile. Almost. "Names Michael, pleasure to meet you."

That's when it happened. A shift. A man on the other side of me had been watching too long, smiling too wide. He leaned in, reeking of cheap liquor and bad intentions. "Hey beautiful, you don't need to waste your time with him. I'll buy your next drink."   .

I shook my head, "Not interested."

But he didn't take no for an answer. His hand brushed my arm, fingers too familiar, and my stomach turned. Before I could tell him again, the storm beside me moved,

Michael

One second, he was a slouched shadow at the bar, the next his hand was around the man's wrist, not cruel, just immovable. His voice came calm, steady. "She said no."

The man tried to laugh it off, tug free. He couldn't. Michael's grip didn't tighten, it simply was.

That's when I felt it.

The air shifted, thickened. His shoulders squared, and something stirred behind his eye. Not just anger. Hunger. The kind of hunger that doesn't end when the fight does. This must be the one they warned me about, the one that is only here for one thing, destruction. HIM.

I froze. The stories were real. Too real. Then another force rose up against it, cutting sharp against that hunger. Controlled, cold, deliberate. He must be Lucian.

"Enough," he said, though the word never left his lips.

Michael exhaled like he'd been holding his breath for hours. The drunk jerked free and stumbled back, muttering curses he didn't mean. He left. The bartender pretended nothing happened.

The tension bled out of the moment as the drunk stumbled off, but it didn't leave me calm. Michael sat back down like nothing had happened, but the storm behind his eyes still lingered, pulsing faint under the surface.

We talked. Small things. Safer things. Names I didn't give, questions he didn't press. He was funny in a dry way, the kind of man who didn't waste words, and for a few minutes I let myself forget the weight in my pocket and the danger outside.

But the drink caught up to him. His eyes went glassier, his sentences heavier, like he was dragging them uphill. He swayed just slightly when he stood.

"I'll walk you to your car," he said.

I hesitated, then nodded. The thought of him at my side was both reassuring and terrifying.

We made it to the hallway before he muttered, "Bathroom. Be right back." He disappeared through the door with the faded MEN sign. And that's when I made the mistake.

I told myself it wasn't worth the wait. That I didn't need him to walk me out. That I could handle a parking lot on my own. So, I pushed through the bar's double doors into the night.

The cold slapped me sober. And then I saw him. The drunk. Waiting.

He grinned when he spotted me, teeth glinting in the glow of the neon beer sign. "Thought you could brush me off, huh?"

Before I could turn back, his hand clamped around my wrist, yanking me toward the alley. My pulse spiked. I clawed at him, shoved, cursed, but he was bigger, angrier, and more sober than he'd looked inside.

We made it two blocks before the footsteps caught us. Heavy. Purposeful. I spun—and my stomach dropped.

It wasn't Michael.

The same body, yes. But the eyes were different. Colder. Calculated.

Lucian.

"Let her go," *he said, voice low, dangerous.*

The drunk sneered, then laughed, dragging me tighter against him. "Or what? You'll fall over? You're drunker than I am."

Lucian tilted his head, studying him like a puzzle he already knew the answer to. "Last chance."

The man didn't take it. He swung.

Lucian blocked, countered, drove him back with sharp, efficient movements, no wasted motion, no wasted breath. But the drunk wasn't alone. A second shadow stepped from the dark, pipe in hand, and before Lucian could turn, it cracked against his skull.

He staggered. For a second, I saw him falter, knees dipping, eyes losing focus. My chest seized.

And then it happened.

The air thickened. A weight pressed down, not from one, but from all of them. I felt it like a vibration in my teeth, in the metal of the brooch, in the space between heartbeats.

Michael's fury. Lucian's precision. Something else, darker, heavier, rising. Not one. Not two. All of them.

The fight ended in seconds. Blows landed faster than I could follow. Bones snapped like dry sticks, bodies crumpled. One man screamed. The other didn't get the chance. Then silence.

Lucian straightened, blood dripping from his temple, breath steady again. His eyes flicked to me, sharp and knowing.

"You saw it," he said. Not a question.

I swallowed hard. "What was that?"

He stepped closer, close enough that I could feel the warning in his presence. "You'll keep quiet. Forget tonight. Leave New York. While you still can."

I should have run then. Should have listened. But I didn't.

(Present)

The memory dissolved, ripped away by the jolt of the truck hitting another rock. My eyes snapped open, the taste of copper thick on my tongue. The night outside was a blur of black trees and dirt road, the headlights cutting just far enough ahead to remind me how far we were from anyone who could hear me scream.

Almost forty-eight hours. I'd stopped trying to count by the hour. Time blurred when you were drugged, beaten, dragged from one dark room to another. My body ached in places I didn't even know had nerves. My wrists burned raw against the zip ties, plastic biting every time the truck swayed.

Two men sat in the front, silhouettes against the dash glow. Marco wasn't with them. He didn't have to be. His men were enough, their clipped Spanish mutters carrying over the rattle of the truck, sharp words I couldn't quite catch but knew weren't about me.

The compound was close. I felt it in my bones before I saw it, the change in the air, the way the trees thinned, the faint glow of floodlights in the distance. My stomach clenched, cold and heavy.

The truck slowed, grinding over gravel. Ahead, I saw the gates, tall steel, barbed wire curling along the top like a crown. Men with rifles slung over their shoulders leaned against the posts, their faces washed pale in the yellow light.

My heart pounded harder, but I forced myself to breathe steadily. If I showed fear, they'd feed on it. If I showed defiance, they'd break me faster. The trick was balance, stay quiet, stay alive, wait for the crack in the armor.

The passenger glanced back at me once, his eyes flat and uninterested, like I was already marked property. Then he turned forward again, murmuring into his radio. The gates groaned, opening wider, swallowing us whole.

I let my head fall back against the seat and closed my eyes, just for a second. Not to rest. Not to surrender. But to picture those sky-blue starburst eyes again.

We started moving again. It felt like I was going to be sick. All the memories here. Forced to play house with man whose ego could fill up Texas.

The truck lurched to a stop, dust rising in the headlights and curling through the night air like smoke. A man yanked the door open before the engine was even cut, barking at me in Spanish I half-understood. Didn't matter, I knew what "out" sounded like in any language.

I slid down from the bench seat, my legs trembling more from exhaustion than fear. Gravel bit into my bare feet. The air smelled of diesel, sweat, and salt. The compound sat close enough to the coast that I could almost hear the waves beneath the chorus of cicadas.

The floodlights washed everything in harsh yellow: high walls strung with wire, squat concrete buildings, armed men drifting like shadows between them. It wasn't chaos, it was organized, efficient, like a machine that had learned to breathe.

One of them shoved me forward. I stumbled but caught myself. I refused to give them the satisfaction of watching me crawl.

The main house loomed ahead, larger than the rest, its windows black behind bars. A balcony stretched across the second floor, and for a moment I thought I saw movement. Someone watching. Him. Marco.

They pushed me through a metal door that groaned on its hinges. Inside, the air turned heavy, thicker with mildew and the faint copper tang of old blood. The hallway was narrow, concrete sweating under the humidity, the fluorescent bulbs overhead buzzing like insects.

My heart kicked harder with every step, but I forced my breathing to stay even. Don't let them see it. Don't give them anything.

At the end of the hall, a room waited. A chair bolted to the floor. Straps. A bucket in the corner that told me people had been left here long enough to need it.

One of the guards smiled as if he'd read my thoughts. He gestured to the chair. "Sit."

I didn't move. Not yet. I lifted my chin instead, even when they shoved me down. The straps bit into my wrists again, leather this time, not plastic. Stronger. Smarter.

The door opened behind me. Boots clicked against the concrete, slower, heavier. A man who never needed to rush.

Marco stepped into the light. He hadn't changed. Crisp white shirt. Rings that glinted as he adjusted his cuffs. A smile so smooth it felt like oil sliding across water.

"Madison," he said, drawing out the name like it was both a greeting and a punishment. "Welcome home."

He paced a slow circle around me, boots clicking steady with each step. "I told myself I'd let you run. Let you burn off that foolishness until you came back on your own. But then I saw you." His voice hardened, almost imperceptibly. "On his arm." He stopped in front of me, crouched low, elbows balanced on his knees so our faces nearly touched.

His smile was calm, but his eyes burned with a cold, restrained fury.

"You've always been predictable, Madison. Soft eyes for men who look like they can save you. But you know the truth, don't you?" His fingers brushed my jawline, forcing my head up when I tried to turn away. "No one saves you from me. No one ever has."

I clenched my teeth. Saying nothing was the only power I had left.

Marco chuckled, straightening. "Ah, silence. That worries me. Quiet women are dangerous women." He slid his ringed hand along the back of the chair as he circled behind me again. "So, tell me... where is it?"

The brooch. Always the brooch.

"I don't know what you're talking about," I said, voice hoarse but steady.

He leaned down behind my ear, his breath warm against my skin. "Lies sound like glass when they break. You'll shatter soon enough."

He nodded, and one of his men stepped forward, setting a tray down on the steel table by the wall. I didn't have to look to know what was on it. Syringes. Pliers. Straps.

Marco stayed close, his shadow falling over me. "We'll start small. A question, an answer, and this ends. Refuse me..." He gestured lazily toward the tray. "And my men will help me loosen your tongue."

He returned to my line of sight, crouching again, voice low, intimate. "Tell me, Madison. Where. Is. My. Brooch?"

I swallowed the taste of blood and forced my lips into the barest hint of a smile. "If you have to ask... you've already lost it."

His eyes narrowed, the first crack in his perfect mask.

And in that moment, for all the fear crushing my ribs, I knew one thing: Marco could cage me, break me, bleed me, but I would never hand him the satisfaction of surrender.

The Devil's Coordinates

(Michael's POV)

Z's fingers never stopped moving over the keys, even as she shot me that grin, sharp enough to cut glass.

"Yes, *we*," she said. "You think you going to storm Puerto Rico blind? You need me. And you know it."

I frowned. "This isn't a group trip."

Lucian's voice slid in first, steady and sharp. *She's right. We'll need her eyes on the ground, we can't afford to go in deaf.*

Jace followed, anxious. *I don't like it, Michael. She's not a fighter. She's not-*

"She's a survivor," Z cut in, like she heard him anyways. Her eyes didn't leave the screen. And she's smarter than any of you when it comes to firewalls and flight logs. Barceloneta's crawling with cartel money, and I just found the threads. Cargo routes. Storage manifest. If Madison's there, she's tied up in this mess tighter than any chain.

"I don't drag civilians into this," I said finally.

Z leaned back in her chair, spinning lazily before letting it creak to a stop. "Funny. I don't remember asking for permission. You came to me, remember? That makes this my job too."

Lucian murmured low. *She'll come, whether we say yes or no. Better to have her close where we can watch her back.*

Jace groaned. *This is insane.*

Maybe it was. But the cursor on her screen blinked over and address, coordinates in neat, brutal numbers. And for the first time since Madison was taken, I felt the ground tilt beneath me toward something that looked like a path.

Z's grin sharpened. "Pack a bag, old man. Barceloneta's waiting."

Oh, don't forget, Puerto rice isn't just cartel turf. You'll be swimming in every alphabet soup agency's backyard. DEA, FBI, hell, even Homeland's got eyes there.

"Good thing I don't answer to any of them," I muttered, slinging the strap of my bag over my shoulder.

She finally looked up, grin sharp. "Yeah. That's what scares me."

Her goodbye was short and sweet. A quick kiss and a promise not to get into any trouble. Yeah, like she's going to keep that promise.

We made our way down to my bike. I threw my leg over and Z mimicked without hesitation. Couldn't tell we've spent hours together could you. The bike roared to life under me.

The city peeled away in streaks of gray and steel, horns blaring as I carved through lanes that weren't meant to exist. Z clung tight, helmet down, but I could feel her watching the way I rode, not reckless, never reckless. Calculated. Every shift of weight, every downshift, every narrow squeeze between cabs was a language only people like me spoke.

Bridges flashed by under our tires, the East River splitting open beneath us, wind cutting sharp against exposed skin. Neon died out the further we pushed, replaced by the skeletal glow of warehouses and the forgotten sprawl of the docks. Z didn't say a word the whole ride, but her silence wasn't fear. It was trust. This was nothing new to her. She'd ridden with me before, back when I wasn't sure if I'd see another sunrise.

I leaned low into a curve, sparks flying as the peg kissed asphalt, and felt her grip tighten. Not out of panic. Not surprise. Just the instinctive trust of someone who knew exactly what kind of man she was riding with.

By the time we cleared the last stretch of highway, the city had bled into nothing but dark stretches of road and the smell of jet fuel drifting on the wind.

The airstrip came into view an hour later, private, fenced, faceless. Just another patch of concrete the government pretends doesn't exist. But I knew better. I'd flown from strips like this all over the world.

The guards at the gate didn't hesitate. One glance at the badge I slid across and their whole posture snapped straight, eyes wide, shoulders square, like they'd just been reminded the devil doesn't always come with horns.

Z only smirked, brushing past them with a roll of her eyes. "Told you," She muttered under her breath. "You're not just a ghost, you're their ghost."

Lucian's voice stirred low in the back of my skull. *That wasn't fear Michael, that was recognition. They know exactly who and what we are.*

Jace followed, uneasy but sharper now. *Yeah...and that's the problem. They look at us like we're not a man. Like we're a weapon they can point and fire.*

After the little show at the gate, we hopped back on and drove a way till we pulled up to a huge metal building.

The hangar doors groaned open as we rolled in, the bike's growl echoing against steel beams and corrugated walls. Fluorescent lights buzzed overhead, cutting strips of white across the polished floor where a sleek black jet waited, nose pointed toward the night.

The air inside was thick with jet fuel and cold steel. The smell of work, of missions that never made it into headlines. Two ground crew in coveralls stopped what they were doing, eyes flicking from the bike to me. Recognition hit first, then posture. Backs straight. Eyes down. Not fear. Not surprise. Reverence.

I killed the engine, the silence hitting harder than the roar. Z slid off behind me, pulling her helmet free. She didn't look around, didn't have to. She'd seen this dance before. The way men twice my size avoided meeting my eyes. The way they saluted without saluting, because this wasn't the kind of place you showed open respect.

"Still dramatic as hell," she muttered under her breath, shaking her head like a sister watching a brother walk back into bad habits.

Boots clanged on metal steps as an officer in black fatigues approached. No rank on his chest, no name. Just the kind of man built to vanish into shadows. He stopped two paces short of me. "Plane's fueled. Flight plan is clear. Destination logged under Phoenix Protocol."

Phoenix. They always had names. Birds, storms, gods. Dressing up murder in mythology.

I signed nothing. Shook no hands. Just walked past him toward the steps of the jet. He didn't stop me. He wouldn't dare.

Lucian's voice was low, steady. *This isn't new, Michael. This is home. You know it.*

Jace's came softer, uneasy. *Yeah, but look at them. They don't see us as a man. They see the thing in the file. The one they built.*

I didn't answer. HIM was still gone, a hollow in the back of my skull where the weight used to sit. And somehow, that emptiness felt louder in here than it did anywhere else.

Z followed close, her boots lighter on the steel steps. She didn't flinch when we passed another set of guards, didn't blink when they shifted their rifles against their shoulders. This was her world too, in a way. She'd just never had to bleed for it.

Inside, the jet was stripped down, leather seats, humming consoles, no windows wide enough to offer comfort. This wasn't built for luxury. This was built to move ghosts across oceans.

Z dropped into a seat like she'd done it a hundred times, pulling a tablet from her bag before the engines even whined. "Barceloneta's waiting," she said, not even looking at me. "Try not to get sentimental."

I sat across from her, the vibration of the turbines bleeding into my bones, steady as a heartbeat. The cabin lights dimmed, and for a moment I caught my reflection in the black glass of the bulkhead. Not a man. Not a monster. Just something in between.

And when the jet rolled forward, climbing into the night, I realized the scariest part wasn't that HIM was missing. It was that I missed him.

(Mindscape)

The hum of the engines bled into the dark, vibrating through the cabin and into my bones. My eyes were shut, body slumped against the leather seat, but I wasn't sleeping. Not really. I was inside — at the table.

Jace leaned forward, nervous energy radiating off him, fingers drumming against the surface that wasn't really there. *I don't like this. He should've been here. By now. The apartment, the Olds, the guards. That's when he pushes through. That's when he takes over. So, where the hell is he?*

Lucian sat back, arms folded, gaze sharp as ever. *You're not wrong. Silence from HIM isn't balance. It's fracture. Like a wheel missing a spoke. We've relied on him, whether we wanted to admit it or not. He's the hunger that never falters. The blade none of us wanted to wield but always could.*

I sat between them, the weight of it sinking in, heavier than the jet itself. *You think I haven't felt it? That quiet pressing down? I used to curse him every damn time he clawed his way up, but now... now it's worse. Because I'm waiting. And he's not coming.*

Jace swallowed, his voice smaller. *Yeah. And maybe I hate saying it, but I miss him. The noise. The pressure. At least then we weren't alone in here. At least then we knew what to expect.*

Lucian's eyes shifted to me, steady and cold. *Better the devil you know, Michael. With HIM, I could push back. Control the edge. This silence? This absence? I can't fight what isn't here.*

For a long moment, none of us spoke. The hum of the engines carried on above us, but in the mindscape, it was just the three of us at that table, and the empty chair at the end.

I looked at it, jaw tight, chest heavy. *You're right. I miss him too.*

Jace finally broke the silence, voice low. *So, what happens if he doesn't come back? What if this is it? Just us?*

Lucian's eyes narrowed. *Then we adapt. We always do. HIM's rage made us fast, violent, untouchable but it also made us sloppy. Reckless. Maybe without him, we sharpen. Cut cleaner.*

I shook my head. *Don't fool yourself. You've felt it. Every time the walls closed in, every time the odds stacked too high it was HIM that tipped the scale. We're alive because he was always willing to go further than we could stomach.*

Neither of them argued. Couldn't.

The chair sat there, silent, heavy.

Jace shifted uncomfortably, running a hand through his hair. *Feels wrong. Like holding our breath, waiting for a punch that never lands. I don't trust it.*

Lucian leaned forward now, elbows on the table, tone harder. *Then we prepare. For Madison. For Marco. For what's waiting in Barceloneta. With or without HIM, we move forward. Hesitation gets us killed.*

I stared at the chair a moment longer, then pushed myself back, rising to my feet. *Fine. Then we carry on.*

The table dissolved around us, mindscape fading until there was only the hum of engines, the press of leather against my shoulders, and the faint vibration of flight beneath my boots.

(Jace's POV)

The engines droned steady, a low vibration threading through the cabin. Michael's head was tipped back against the seat, finally letting himself drift. Lucian had gone quiet too, not from discipline, he just didn't care for long flights unless there was a drink and a woman waiting on the other end.

Me taking control…like this happens more than you think. Michael runs himself into the ground trying to control everything, more like trying to keep me safe if I'm being honest with myself.

I appreciate everything he does, but sometimes he's a little overbearing. So, when I get to have control back it's refreshing.

Z didn't even glance up from her tablet when my focus shifted. She'd known the second I stepped forward. She always did. That was the thing about her, she didn't just see Michael, she saw us. All of us.

"Jace," she said evenly, not a question.

"Yeah," I answered, leaning forward, elbows on my knees. "He needed rest. And Lucian's not exactly built for quiet reflection."

That earned me the smallest smirk from her. "No argument there."

Her fingers flicked across the tablet, pulling up strings of cargo logs, charter manifests, encrypted routing notes. She finally slid it across to me. "Take a look. Tell me what's off."

I scanned the lines once, then again slower. Numbers, times, names. Most people would see nothing but clutter. But I'd always been the one to catch the seams. The stitch out of place. The detail no one else had the patience for. "Here," I said, tapping the screen. "This flight path loops wider than it should. Adds an hour without reason. And this cargo code? It doesn't match the manifests around it. It's cleaner. Too clean. Somebody's hiding something in plain sight."

Z leaned back, arms crossing, her eyes never leaving me. "That's what I like about you, Jace. You don't just see the play; you see the trick under it."

I didn't smile. Not really. But I nodded once. "Michael will strategize the strike. Lucian will make the mess when it comes. But me? I make sure we don't walk blind into it."

For the first time in a long while, I felt seen. Not as the background voice. Not as hesitation. But as part of the whole.

We talked for hours, the drone of the engines steady beneath us. Z kept the tablet glowing between us, sometimes sliding it over for me to scan, sometimes just letting the silence stretch. It wasn't awkward.

With her, it never was. She knew when to push, when to let things breathe. I pointed out patterns, little inconsistencies in the manifests and flight logs. She smirked each time I caught one, muttering, "Knew you'd see it," like it was just confirmation of what she already believed.

Hours blurred past that way, calm and steady, until the soft chime overhead broke the rhythm. The seatbelt light clicked on, and the jet shifted under us, nose angling down.

Z closed the tablet, locking it with a flick. "Descent," she said, her voice back to business, sharp and clear.

Marco – The Wolf's Den

The compound never slept.

Floodlights cut the night into sharp angles, guards shifting in practiced rhythm along the perimeter. The jungle pressed close beyond the wire, its song smothered by diesel engines, the grind of boots on gravel, the occasional crackle of radio chatter. All of it mine.

I stood on the balcony of the main house, leaning against the iron railing, a glass of rum untouched in my hand. Below, men moved like pieces on a board, every step familiar. Order. Structure. Fear. I built it that way.

Inside, Madison was waiting. They'd strapped her down where I told them to. Not too tight, not too loose — enough for her to feel the bite of restraint, enough to remind her that comfort was a memory she no longer owned.

The scar along my throat burned faint in the cold breeze, a reminder and a promise. My family's blood runs deep in this place. Her defiance, her theft, her running… all of it was a stain I intended to wash out in full.

The brooch had been hers once, through her grandmothers' hands. But desperation sold it to me, or rather to my family. Payment for medicine her mother couldn't afford. A debt paid in gold and stone.

She never wore it, not after that. But she never forgot it either. I saw it in her eyes every time the light caught it, every time I let her glimpse it as mine.

Because that's what it was now. Mine. Claimed fair, kept permanent. She could run from me, spit curses at me, bleed under my roof, but nothing would change that truth.

It would have stayed that way except for one drunken night. I allowed myself to feel vulnerable. That's when she was able to bribe a guard, one that is no longer employed by me, and somehow make it to New York City. That's where she met him.

Michael.

I said his name like a curse, low, just for myself. He was no ordinary rival, and I knew it. Men like him didn't just exist, they were built, sharpened by hands unseen. A ghost wearing a soldier's skin.

And if he came here, if he dared step into my den, I would show him what it meant to steal from a wolf.

I raised the glass at last, letting the rum burn slow down my throat. Behind me, footsteps approached, measured, careful. My second-in-command. He knew not to speak until I allowed it.

"Bring her," I said. My voice carried across the night like a blade drawn slowly.

They obeyed. They always did. A few minutes later, she was in front of me, dragged into the room by two of my men. Straps cut into her wrists, ankles raw, but her chin still lifted. Defiant. That was Madison. Even caged, even broken down to the bone, she burned like she thought fire alone could melt steel.

I let her stand there, forced on her knees at last, while I stayed seated. I didn't need to tower over her. The weight of me sitting calm was enough.

"You hate me," I said simply, swirling the rum in my glass. "I've seen it in your eyes since the first time I showed you the brooch. The day you realized what your grandmother gave up. What she sold to keep your mother breathing."

Her jaw clenched, eyes narrowing, but she didn't answer.

I leaned forward just enough, letting the light catch across the scar on my throat. "Every time you looked at it, you hated me. And yet you never left. Do you know why?"

I let the silence stretch, watching her fight with herself. The guards shifted, uncomfortable, but I didn't look at them. Only at her.

"Because hate binds tighter than love. Love lets go. Hate never does. That is why you stayed. That is why you'll always come back. Because I am in your blood now, Madison. And there is no running from that."

Her breath hitched, just slightly, but I saw it. That crack, the kind I had built everything on.

Control wasn't about chains or bullets. It was about memory. And I owned every piece of hers that mattered.

Her silence stretched, a stone wall between us. She kept her chin high, eyes burning, but her lips stayed closed.

I swirled the rum once, slow, then set it down. The calm left my voice.

"Where is it?" I snapped, the words striking like a whip. "Where is my brooch?"

Nothing. Not a word.

My chair scraped against the floor as I stood, the scar across my throat burning with every heartbeat. "Do you think you can defy me, Madison? Do you think he—" I spat the word like venom, "Michael—can protect you from me?!"

Her silence mocked me more than her words ever could. My hand shot up, palm open, every man in the room knowing what came next.

She flinched, just barely, but then her voice cut sharp through the air.

"Go ahead," she hissed. "It was your favorite pastime when your little psychological games didn't work on me."

The room froze.

For a moment, the only sound was the hum of the lights above, the breath in my chest. My men stared, waiting. She had handed me the strike she expected, begged for it in her defiance.

But I didn't swing. Not yet.

I lowered my hand slowly, every muscle trembling with the fury I swallowed back. A wolf didn't bite every time it bared its teeth. Sometimes, the waiting was worse.

"You'll talk," I said finally, voice low again, more dangerous for its restraint. "Not today, not tomorrow. But soon. And when you do, it won't be with that fire in your eyes. It will be with tears."

I leaned close, close enough for her to feel my breath. "Because the brooch is mine, Madison. Always was. Always will be. And when I have it again, you'll understand what it means to belong to me."

Her breath came sharp through her nose, chin still raised though the straps dug deep into her wrists. She hadn't broken. Not yet.

I straightened, pacing a slow circle around the chair. My boots rang against the floor, each step measured, deliberate. "Do you know why you're here, Madison? Not because you ran. Not because you hid with him. But because you dared to touch what was mine. The brooch. Me. Everything about you belongs here. To me."

Still nothing. No words.

I clenched my jaw, heat building under my skin. "Answer me."

Her silence was louder than any scream.

The glass in my hand cracked under my grip. I hurled it to the wall, shards scattering across the concrete. "WHERE IS IT?!" My voice shook the room, making the guards shift uneasy at the door.

Madison's lips pressed together, refusing me.

I slammed both palms onto the armrests of her chair, leaning down until my scarred throat hovered inches from her face. "You will tell me, Madison. You will break. Do you hear me? You always do."

She flinched again when my hand lifted, palm open, hovering above her cheek. I saw it, that flicker of instinct, the recoil she tried to hide. It fed me.

But then her voice came — low, bitter, sharp as a blade dragged across glass.

"Go ahead," she hissed. "Like I said before, it was always your favorite pastime. Every time your little mind games didn't work on me, you used your fists instead. Go on, Marco. Be predictable."

The room went dead still.

My hand trembled midair, not from weakness — from fury. From the audacity. She'd given me the strike she wanted, baited it out like a dare.

Slowly, I lowered it, knuckles whitening. Then I snapped my fingers.

Two guards stepped forward, eyes darting between us.

"Teach her," I said, my voice low, venom wrapped in steel. "Show her what silence costs. Show her what defiance earns."

They hesitated. Everyone hesitated when it came to her.

"NOW!" I roared, the sound ripping through the chamber like thunder.

The guards moved in, hesitation lingering on their faces. I could see it, they didn't want to touch her, not unless I forced the issue.

Madison's lips curled into the faintest shadow of a smile. Defiance. Even bruised, strapped down, staring into my fury, she smiled.

"You can have me beaten all you want," she said, her voice steady enough to slice through the room. "Have your lackeys torture me day in and day out. But you'll never get the brooch."

My jaw clenched.

She leaned forward as far as the restraints allowed, eyes burning into mine. "But that's the least of your worries." A pause, deliberate, every word sharpened like a knife. "He's coming for me. And I don't mean Michael."

The words cracked across the chamber like lightning. I froze. For the first time that night, I froze.

The guards glanced at each other, unease showing in their posture. They didn't understand, not fully — but I did. She wasn't bluffing. She believed it.

My scar burned hot under the lights. The taste of iron filled my mouth though I hadn't bitten my tongue. She was speaking of the thing I'd only glimpsed in fragments, the shadow behind Michael's eyes, the monster restrained but never gone.

I snarled, low and dangerous, masking the flicker of unease her words struck. "Then let him come," I spat. "This is my den. And wolves don't fear ghosts."

I turned sharply to the guards, fury snapping back into command. "Do it. Make her remember whose house she's in."

The guards finally obeyed, stepping in close. One grabbed Madison by the shoulders, shoving her back against the chair. The other drew a fist, hesitating only long enough to glance at me.

"Don't stop," I said, voice like a blade dragged across stone. "Not until she forgets how to smile."

Her jaw set, defiance still glowing in her eyes. That was the last thing I saw before I turned, the first crack of knuckles against flesh echoing behind me.

I didn't need to watch. I'd seen enough of her broken before. The pain was never what bent her, it was the repetition. Pain stacked on pain until even fire forgot how to burn.

I walked the corridor slowly, letting their fists and her muffled cries fade into the hum of the compound. Each step cooled the rage in me, settling it back into the calm I wore like a second skin. By the time I reached the stairwell, my breathing was even again.

That's when I heard it.

"Señor."

My second-in-command appeared at the top of the stairs, eyes sharp, words clipped. He didn't waste time. "We've spotted a jet. Small, unmarked. Landed on the strip outside Barceloneta."

I stopped, fingers brushing the railing.

A jet? Here?

My scar throbbed with heat, the kind that came with memory. Michael. Or whatever shadow walked with him.

I nodded once, slow, deliberate. "Keep eyes on it. Quiet. No mistakes. If it's him..." My mouth curled into something between a smile and a snarl. "...let him make the first move."

My man bowed his head and vanished back down the hall. I had taken no more than three steps toward the stairs before I stopped. Her words still rang in my head, sharper than the sound of fists meeting flesh. He's coming for me. And I don't mean Michael.

I turned back.

The guards were doing their work, knuckles stained red, Madison's head snapping with each blow. She was bleeding, but her eyes still burned through the swelling.

"Enough," I said.

The word hit harder than their fists. Both men froze, backing off at once. Madison slumped in the chair, breath ragged, one eye swollen half-shut, but that fire was still there.

I crouched in front of her, slow, deliberate, forcing her to meet my gaze.

"You think words will save you?" My tone was calm again, low, venom laced with silk. "That ghost you cling to, the one hiding behind Michael's skin — you think he's the storm on the horizon?"

She spit blood at the floor, a crimson smear against the concrete.

I smiled. Then I lied.

"My second just informed me," I said softly, almost kindly, "that we apprehended your man. Michael. The ghost, the soldier, whatever you think he is. He landed on my island, and now he's mine."

Her eyes widened, just barely — there's the look I yearn for.

I leaned closer, whispering against her ear, the rum on my breath hot against her cheek. "So, tell me, Madison, what happens to the ghost when wolves have him by the throat?"

I straightened, snapping my fingers for the guards to step back entirely. She needed the space to feel the weight of my words. To drown in them.

I didn't need chains to hold her anymore. I had something stronger. Doubt.

Unwelcomed

(Jace's POV)

The jet tilted, nose angling down, the hum of the engine shifting in pitch. The seatbelt light glowed overhead, but I was already strapped in, already awake.

The clouds broke, and Barceloneta spread out below—lights scattered along the coastline, the black stretch of jungle pressing around it, the ocean gleaming silver under the moon. From up here it almost looked peaceful. Almost.

But I knew better.

Michael had walked these streets before, and because he has, I had. The memories weren't mine, not really, but they lived in me all the same. Gunfire in narrow alleys. Blood in the gutters. The echo of Marco's voice in the dark, taunting from the shadows.

I flexed my fingers against the armrest, steadying my breath. This place wasn't just another stop on the map. Barceloneta remembered us as much as we remembered it.

Z's voice cut through the drone of the cabin. "You're too quiet. Makes me nervous."

I glanced over. She was buckled in, tablet off for once, eyes fixed on me instead of the screen.

"Just thinking," I said.

"That's your job," she shot back, lips twitching like it was half a joke, half-truth. "Michael strategizes, Lucian drinks his way through the noise, HIM...well HIM isn't here.

That leaves you. The one who notices that smallest of details.

I held her stare a moment before nodding. "Noticed something, yeah. The city doesn't look any different, but it feels…heavier. Like its waiting for us."

She smirked faintly, but there was no humor in her eyes. "Good. Means you're paying attention. This place isn't just Marco's playground. It's his home turf. And nothing bites harder than a cornered animal."

I leaned back as the landing gear dropped, the rumble shaking through the floor. "Then let's remind him that animals bleed too."

The heels slammed down, a heavy jolt that rattled through the cabin. The engines roared, brakes grinding against the strip as the jet slowed hard, the night outside streaking past in flashes of light.

Through the narrow window, I caught the glow of floodlights sweeping across the tarmac, the silhouettes of armed men posted at the edge of the field. Marco's eyes no doubt. Watching. Measuring.

Z unbuckled the second we rolled to a stop, already reaching for her bag. Her movements were sharp, practiced. No nerves. That's what I admired about her-she never rattled.

Michael didn't stir. He was still sunk deep, lost in the silence where HIM should've been. Lucian said nothing either. That left me, again.

I rose, checked the weight of the knife at my hip, then glanced at Z. "This is it. No mistakes."

She smirked, though her eyes stayed hard. "Please. If I wanted safe and easy, I would've stayed home.

The door hissed open, and warm Puerto Rican air flooded the cabin, thick with salt and diesel. The kind of air that carried memories whether you wanted them or not.

Barceloneta.

Every step down the stairwell, I felt it pressing in – the weight of a city, which remembered us as much as we remembered it.

Behind me Michael stirred. His presence getting stronger, sharper now, the strategist awakes.

Jace, he said, *I can take it from here.*

I stopped on the stairs, one boots planted on steel, the other already hanging over the night. I didn't turn. *No. Not yet.*

Silence stretched between us, the engines ticking as they cooled.

I mean it, I continued. *You'll have your time soon enough. But right now, you stay ready. If Marco's men are waiting, we don't need you or Lucian. We need someone who can read between the lines.*

Z glanced back at me, as if she could see the internal conversation I just had, a flicker of approval in her eyes. She didn't say a word. She didn't have to.

Michael exhaled, the faintest ghost of a nod. *Then make damn sure you don't miss a thing.*

I tightened my grip on the railing, scanning the floodlights below. *Don't worry. I won't.*

Boots hit the tarmac, the humid night wrapping around me like a shroud. The salt air clung to my skin, heavy with the stink of fuel.

Floodlights snapped brighter, cutting across the strip. Shapes moved at the edges.

They stepped into the light in twos, rifles loose in their hands but not low enough to be friendly. Their eyes swept the jet, then fixed on us."

Z shifted her bag higher on her shoulder, posture calm, deliberate. I matched her pace, steady but unshaken.

One of them barked in Spanish, words clipped, a demand we both understood without needing a translation. Stop. Identify. Submit.

I didn't stop.

I lifted my chin, gaze locked on the one who'd spoken. "We're expected," I said flat, certain. No explanation. No permission asked. Just truth spoken like a blade.

The man frowned, glancing at the others. A ripple of uncertainty ran through them. They weren't ready for someone who didn't posture, didn't flinch.

I felt Michael's presence stir again, voice low, measured. *Jace...*

I've got this, I snapped back. Never breaking eye contact with the guard.

The silence stretched, thick as the air, before the man finally gestured with his rifle, a signal. Two broke off to circle around, searching the jet. The others stayed planted, staring us down.

Z smirked faintly; her voice low enough for only me. "You play a good wolf, Jace."

"Not playing," I said, "Just watching."

And I kept watching, every detail sharp – the way one man's finger twitched near the trigger, the faint shake in another's stance, the scared knuckles on the one blocking or path.

The man in front finally lowered his rifle just enough to step forward. His boots struck heavy against the pavement, each step deliberate. He stopped a foot from me, the sour stink of cigarettes and swat rolling off him.

"Detenganse," he growled, jabbing the barrel of his rifle against my chest. Not a warning. A command.

Z shifted beside me, weight moving just enough that I knew her hand was near her blade. Michael's voice cut low, quiet but sharp. *"Jace, now."*

I said I've got this, I muttered, never taking my eyes off the man in front of me.

The guard sneered, pressing harder with the rifle. Testing me. Daring me.

I moved.

Not fast – fast gets sloppy. Precise. My hand snapped up, palm slamming against the barrel, twisting it sideways as my other drove into his throat. The air whooshed out of him, his grip faltering. Before he could recover, I wrenched the rifle from his hands, spun it once, and aimed it right back as his chest.

The floodlights hummed, the other mend didn't freeze. They surged.

Z was already moving, her blade flashing in the glow as she slashed across the first barrel, sparks jumping. I fired a single shot into the ground, forcing two of them to scatter, but another swung the butt of his rifle at my head. I ducked low, and drove my elbow into his gut, then cracked the stock across his jaw. He dropped like a sack of stones.

Moore boots, more shadows spilling in from the edges. It wasn't a search party anymore. It was mob.

"Too many," Z snapped, slashing another man's leg out from under him.

"Then we cut through," I growled, snapping the magazine free from the stolen rifle and hurling it into another man's face. He yelped, staggered – long enough for me to crush his knee sideways.

They pressed tighter, shouting in Spanish, rifles raised but hesitant. Orders were shouted from the back, someone trying to corral the chaos.

Then headlights cut across the strip.

A black truck barreled through the outer gate, tires screeching against the pavement. It spun sideways, skidding to a stop between us and the advancing guards. Doors flew open, rifles out, but not cartel steel — cleaner, sharper. Professional.

"¡Vámonos!" a voice barked from behind the truck's lights.

Z grinned, breathless, shoving her blade back into its sheath. "About time."

I grabbed her arm, and we moved, sprinting low as bullets cracked against the truck's frame. The contact's men fired back, short, controlled bursts, carving a gap.

Michael stirred behind my eyes, voice sharp. *Jace—who is this?*

Does it matter? He's our way out now, I muttered, diving into the open door as Z slid in beside me.

The truck roared forward, gunfire fading behind us as the airstrip vanished into the dark. Z shoved her hair back, her grin sharp despite the chaos.

"Cutting it close, Conner," she said, voice pitched over the engine.

I blinked, glancing at her, then at the man driving. He was older than her by a handful of years, jaw tight, eyes locked on the road, but the resemblance was there. Same sharp features. Same don't-flinch-for-anything energy.

He didn't look back when he answered. "Wasn't exactly invited to the party. You're lucky I was watching the strip."

Z smirked, buckling her harness. "You're always watching."

Michael's voice stirred low behind my eyes. *Who the hell is this?*

Z caught my look and finally said it out loud. "Michael, meet Conner. My brother."

I give her a skeptical look.

Michael cuts in, *she's protecting us.*

Conner took a hard turn, tires squealing as we hit the cracked coastal road. "Older brother," he corrected, still not looking at me. "Don't forget it."

Z rolled her eyes. "Please. By five years, and you still think it makes you smarter."

He snorted, finally cutting a glance back at me in the mirror. His stare was hard, measuring, like he was deciding whether to shoot me or shake my hand. "You the one she keeps getting into trouble for?"

"Depends who you ask," I said evenly.

He didn't smile. But he didn't argue either.

The truck jostled over broken pavement, climbing deeper into the maze of backstreets. The city's glow bled away behind us, replaced by thick jungle shadows pressing close on both sides.

Conner finally spoke again. "We'll be safe soon. Safe house is clean. Nobody gets in without me knowing."

Michael muttered inside, sharp and skeptical. *Nobody's ever really safe here.*

The truck tore down the coastal road, engine growling as Conner weaved through the backstreets. Barceloneta blurred past in fragments — neon signs flickering over shuttered cantinas, stray dogs darting across cracked pavement, locals peeking from behind broken shutters as the headlights swept their windows.

Z sat in the passenger seat, eyes scanning every rooftop and alley like she was wired to the city itself. I sat in the back, Michael's silence heavy behind my eyes, Lucian muttering his usual commentary like static at the edge of thought.

Conner didn't speak much, not until we hit the edge of town and the streetlights thinned into jungle. "Roads are dirt from here," he said, voice low, steady. "That keeps Marco's boys nervous. They don't like chasing where headlights die."

The truck jolted as we hit the rutted path, shadows swallowing us whole. The ocean smell faded, replaced by damp earth and the musk of thick trees pressing in tight on both sides.

Z glanced at him, then back at me. "Still think you know every inch of this city, huh?"

Conner's knuckles flexed against the wheel, but his eyes never left the road. "Knowing it is the only reason we're still breathing."

Nobody argued. The drive stretched longer than it probably was, the night pressing down on all of us until the jungle finally broke open into a clearing. Ahead, concrete walls crouched low, a single light burning above a steel door.

The safe house wasn't much — concrete walls, barred windows, and a rusted generator groaning in the corner. But the way Conner carried himself inside told me it was safer than anything else in this city.

He dropped a map onto the scarred wooden table, tracing lines with a calloused finger. "Marco's been shifting product through Barceloneta's north pier. Cargo in, cash out. But he's moving more men than usual. Someone spooked him." His eyes flicked to me, sharp. "My guess? You."

I didn't flinch. Z leaned against the wall, arms folded, watching him with that half-smirk that always said she was three steps ahead.

Conner kept going. "His compound's locked down tight, tighter than I've ever seen it. Guards on rotation, checkpoints doubled. He's expecting trouble. If Madison's there, she's buried deep."

The words landed heavy, but steady. Information like this was the kind of weight you could build a plan around.

Conner straightened, looking at me hard. "If you're going in, you'll need more than firepower. You'll need precision. Marco's not sloppy anymore."

I gave a short nod, but before I could answer, Z pushed off the wall, her gaze shifting my way. "Noted," she said to her brother. Then, lower — so low only I could hear — she added, "It's time to bring Michael back out. You know it."

Her eyes locked on mine, unwavering. She wasn't asking. She was telling me what I already knew but didn't want to admit: this was bigger than me.

Inside, Michael stirred, quiet, measured. Waiting.

I held on a moment longer, fingers tightening against the armrest like I could stall the inevitable. Z's eyes didn't move, didn't blink. She knew.

Inside, the hum of the mindscape stirred — Lucian leaning back, watching, saying nothing for once.

Michael's voice came steady, patiently. *It's time, Jace.*

My jaw clenched. I hated how right he was. Slowly, I exhaled, loosening my grip, letting the weight slide back across the table we all shared.

The shift was instant — familiar, practiced. Michael straightened in the chair, eyes sharper now, movements precise where mine had been steady.

I eased back into the dark, not gone, just quieter. Still there. Still watching.

It was his turn.

Shadows and Steel

(Michael's POV)

The safe house hummed quietly around us, Conner bent over the map, Z leaning back with that smirk that meant she'd already solved three problems I hadn't even seen yet.

I felt the shift coming before it happened. Jace had held the wheel long enough. His grip on the armrest eased, his voice fading into the background like the tide pulling back from the shore.

"It's yours," he muttered in the dark of our mind. *"Don't waste it."*

I sat forward, spine straightening, eyes sharpening on the map. The strategist was awake again.

Z's gaze flicked to me, just for a second. She always knew. Always. "Welcome back," she said low, under her breath, so Conner couldn't hear.

"Never left," I murmured, but she only arched a brow.

Conner traced a finger across the northern pier, his tone clipped. "This is where he's moving his product. Guard rotations here, here, and here. He's doubled security since word got out about the brooch. Madison won't be in the compound's outer cells — too easy. If she's here, she's locked down in the inner wing."

I studied the map, mind already pulling angles, exits, the rhythm of boots, the blind spots. Barceloneta was a web. Marco had built it well. But webs were only as strong as the hands weaving them.

"Perimeter guards rotate every two hours," Conner continued. "But there's a gap, here — between the docks and the southern checkpoint. Three minutes at most. It's enough if you're fast."

"Fast isn't the problem," I said, voice level, eyes still on the map. "Noise is. One mistake and Marco's wolves will swarm the compound before we even reach the gate."

Z pushed off the wall, arms crossed. "Then don't make a mistake."

Lucian's chuckle stirred faint inside. *She talks like she's one of us.*

"She is," I muttered back, then tapped the map. "We move through the pier. Quiet. If we're right, Madison's inside by the time the next rotation hits. If we're wrong…"

Jace's voice, steadier now, floated up from the dark. *Then we adapt. Like always.*

I exhaled through my nose, the faintest nod. He was right.

Conner looked at me sharply, suspicion flickering. "You're not like most men who come here. You don't ask if it's possible. You just decide it will be."

I didn't answer. My hand curled into a fist over the pier marked in ink.

Marco had his den. But I had the hunt.

Conner shoved the map aside and scraped a chair back from the table. "Planning on an empty stomach gets men killed. I'll grab food."

Z smirked. "Still pretending you cook?"

"Still knowing better than to try," he muttered, snatching his jacket from the hook. "There's a place two streets down. Old man still fries chicken like it's a holy calling. Don't burn the safe house down while I'm gone."

The door clicked shut behind him, and the generator hummed on. The silence he left behind was heavier than the map.

Z leaned back, spinning slowly in her chair. "Say it."

I looked up from the map. "Say what?"

"That we don't move tonight."

I exhaled, the weight of the words grinding against my chest. "We don't move tonight."

Her smirk softened, just for a second. "Good. I'd rather not scrape you out of the gutter before I even get to enjoy Puerto Rican coffee."

Lucian lounged in the back of my head, his grin audible. *I'd rather enjoy Puerto Rican rum, but apparently that's not on the itinerary.*

"*Shut up,*" I muttered.

Z's gaze flicked to me, sharp. "HIM?"

"Lucian," I corrected. Her eyebrow arched, like she didn't need the clarification.

The hum of the generator filled the pause. Then she leaned forward, dragging the brooch across the map with one finger like she was drawing blood. "This isn't about firepower. It never was. Marco's got wolves at every corner. You want Madison back, you don't storm. You cut seams until the whole thing collapses."

Jace stirred steady behind my eyes. *She's right. We sharpen now. Watch. Wait. The opening comes later.*

Z glanced at me again, almost reading it. "See? Even your Boy Scout agrees with me."

Lucian snorted. *Please. If the Boy Scout agrees with her, it must be gospel truth.*

I didn't answer. My hand closed over the brooch, pulling it back into my palm. Heavy. Too heavy for what it was.

The door swung open again. Conner dropped a greasy paper bag onto the table, the smell of fried chicken bleeding into the room, cutting through mildew and jet fuel. "Eat," he said simply.

Z grinned, already tearing into it. She shoved a wrapped piece toward me. "Protein. Don't argue."

I didn't. For a moment, it almost felt normal. Almost.

Conner sank into the chair across from me, grease already on his knuckles. "Marco's wolves are twitching," he said through a mouthful. "Rumors are running the dockside. Something spooked him. Not sure if it's you, or if he just thinks it is. Either way, he's tightening the leash."

I chewed slowly, swallowed. "Let him tighten it. The tighter it gets, the louder it snaps when we pull."

Z leaned her cheek into her palm, eyes on me over the rim of a drumstick. "That's the strategist talking."

I didn't argue. She was right.

The grease-stained bag collapsed flat between us, bones and wrappers scattered across the map like markers of a different kind of war. For a moment the safe house smelled like fried chicken instead of mildew and rust, and I let myself sit in it. Quiet. Almost normal.

Conner wiped his hands on a rag, leaned back, and fixed me with that older-brother stare. The kind that wasn't asking for permission, just daring you to lie. "You're not just here for Madison."

I kept my face blank, but Lucian chuckled low inside. *He's got you pegged already.*

Jace muttered steady. *Don't give him anything we don't have to. He's Z's brother, not ours.*

Z cut in before I had to answer. "He doesn't need to explain himself, Conner. You got your part. Let him worry about his."

"His part affects my city," Conner snapped back, his jaw flexing. "If he burns too hot, I'll be the one dragging you out in pieces."

Z smirked, licking grease from her thumb. "Like you've never dragged me anywhere I didn't want to go."

The tension between them crackled sharper than the bulb humming in the corner. I let it ride a moment, then leaned forward, setting both hands on the map. "Enough. We prepare, we rest, we wait. Nobody's burning anything tonight."

That shut them both up.

The generator hummed on. Cicadas rasped outside. Somewhere in the jungle a dog barked once, then stopped. Barceloneta pressed close, listening.

Z pushed her chair back, boots thudding lightly against the concrete. She grabbed a fresh notepad from the desk and a stub of pencil. "Alright, old man. Play teacher. If I'm supposed to be your eyes, show me what I should be looking for."

I raised a brow. "You don't already know?"

Her smirk was sharp, but her eyes were serious. "Of course I know. But I want to see if you see it the same way."

Jace leaned forward inside. *She's testing you. Making sure you're awake. Show her.*

So, I did. I pulled the map back, tapped the pier, then traced the southern checkpoint with my finger. "He's doubled men here, here, and here. Not because it's strong — but because he thinks it's weak. Marco always over-defends the thing he's most afraid of losing."

Z scribbled fast, nodding. "Classic misdirection. So, where's the actual seam?"

I tapped the northern pier again. "Here. One rotation crosses too slow. If we move at the changeover, we've got a window. Three minutes. Maybe less. But it's there."

Lucian hummed, amused. *You always did love cutting it close.*

Z sketched a rough diagram, then circled the pier twice. "You're right. But we're not touching it tonight."

"No," I agreed. "Tonight, we prepare."

She leaned back again, twirling the pencil, eyes sharp on mine. "Then let's prepare."

Conner grunted, pushing up from his chair. "I'll check the perimeter. You two try not to kill each other." He grabbed his rifle and slipped out the back, boots fading against the dirt.

Silence pressed in again. Z didn't fill it this time. She just looked at me, pencil tapping the edge of the map.

"You're quieter than usual," she said at last.

I didn't answer right away. The truth was heavy, bitter. But she always knew.

Finally, I said it. "HIM's still gone."

Her expression didn't shift, but her hand stilled against the paper. "And you hate it."

"Yes."

Jace's voice was steady inside. *We all do.*

Lucian's was softer than usual, almost grudging. *At least when he was loud, we knew where he stood. Silence is worse.*

Z's gaze didn't waver. "Then stop pretending you don't miss him. Own it. You'll need him. Maybe not tonight. But soon."

Her words cut deep because they were true. The silence where HIM should've been pressed harder against my skull, and for the first time I admitted what I hadn't wanted to out loud.

"Yeah, I miss HIM."

The generator coughed, lights flickered and then steadied again. Z flipped her notepad shut, set the pencil down, and stood. "Get some rest, old man. Tomorrow, we start watching. No more running blind."

I leaned back, staring at the brooch glinting faint under the single bulb. Marco had his den. But tonight, I had steel. And shadows. And maybe, if the silence broke, fire.

The safe house settled into a low hum, the generator droning steady in the corner. Conner's boots scraped once outside, then faded into the night. Z shoved away from the desk, rubbing at her eyes, and dropped onto the cot with a groan.

She rolled onto her side, hoodie half-zipped, hair falling across her cheek. "You're not gonna stare at that map all night," she muttered, voice already thick with exhaustion. "Come lie down awhile."

"I should—"

"Not asking," she cut in, eyes closed, hand waving lazily toward the empty space beside her.

I stayed still a moment longer, but my body had other plans. I crossed the room and stretched out on the cot. It groaned under my weight.

Z shifted immediately, sliding in close like it was second nature. Her head tucked against my chest, one arm draped across me, her leg hooked casually over mine. Like I wasn't six-four and covered in scars. Like I was just solid enough to hold her up.

I let out a slow breath, my hand resting against her back. Her breathing steadied, matching the hum of the generator, and the weight of her against me pressed the silence back for the first time in days.

The map, the brooch, the hunt, they'd still be waiting in the morning. Tonight, there was only this.

Sleep came in pieces. The kind where you're never fully gone, but the edge of exhaustion blunts the blades in your head. When I stirred, it was to the faint creak of the front door and the cool rush of dawn air sliding in behind it.

Conner's boots scraped the concrete. He stepped into the room with the same deliberate weight he carried everywhere, eyes sweeping the corners before landing on us.

He didn't say a word. Just stood there a beat, jaw tight, taking in his little sister curled against me like I was the only anchor she trusted.

For a second, I thought he might bark something, remind us this was war, not family time. Instead, he shook his head once, quiet, and set a steaming paper cup of coffee down on the table beside the cold remains of last night's chicken.

"Sun's up," he said low, almost to himself. Then he moved past us, settling by the door with his rifle balanced across his lap, eyes already scanning the tree line outside.

Z didn't stir. Her breath stayed steady.

I let my eyes close again, just for a little longer.

The Cage-HIM

The cage is always the same. Bars that aren't bars. Shadow and iron pressed together, humming with a weight that isn't mine.

I pace. The blood in me says move, break, burn. The Presence just watches. He doesn't glare. Doesn't gloat. He waits like stone waits.

You slammed the bars when they took her, *he says, voice everywhere and nowhere.* If I'd let you out, you'd have painted that apartment red.

Damn right I would've, *I snarl.*

And then? *The question isn't sharp. It's steady, patient.* Three dead. Three left. Madison still gone. You wouldn't have chased. You would have feasted.

My fists curl tight. He's right. I hate it.

You're a storm, *the Presence says.* They are scouts. A storm clears the field. A scout finds the path. If you had gone out there, no one would have led. Not Michael. Not Jace. Not Lucian. Not. You.

I slam my hands against the bars. They don't rattle. They never rattle.

Then what am I for, if not to tear?

The Presence's tone doesn't shift. Calm. Quiet. Final. You are for the moment when tearing is the only way left.

The silence after cuts deeper than chains.

I pace again. The bars never bend, no matter how I slam them. The Presence just watches. Always watching.

You held me back. *I growl.* Every time. Jack, the bikes, the guards at the strip. Why? You stronger than me?

The Presence doesn't bristle. Doesn't rise. His voice is steady, calm, like water shaping stone. Not stronger. Different.

I laugh, bitter, raw. Cryptic bullshit.

You asked, *he says simply.*

I grip the bars tight enough my knuckles split. I've broken everything that ever stood in my way. Michael's walls. Jace's fear. Lucian's pride. But you? You don't move. What the hell are you?

The Presence doesn't answer right away. He lets the silence fill, the kind that makes your rage echo back at you until you choke on it.

Finally, he speaks. I am the weight that keeps the storm from burning the field before the scouts find the path. I am the reason you have a world left to rage in. Without me, you'd have nothing to protect.

The words hit harder than chains. Harder than steel. Because I don't understand him. And I hate what I don't understand.

The bars fade, but they don't open. The Presence doesn't move me forward, not really. He pulls me back.

The mindscape bends, shadows folding until I see a street I know. Puerto Rico. Years ago. My boots on broken pavement, my hands red with the last breath of a man who thought a blade made him a wolf. I remember the rush, the certainty that no one else could have carried us through that night.

The Presence's voice hums steady. Here, you were necessary. Michael was cornered. Jace was too young in the head.

Lucian was blind with arrogance. Without you, Barceloneta would've buried you all.

The memory dissolves. Another takes its place. An alley. Rain slick. Jace young, shoulders tight, fists clenched as three older boys circled him. He thought he had to fight them alone. I was there, I remember surging forward, breaking bones, leaving them bleeding in the gutter.

The Presence speaks again, quieter this time. Here, you weren't needed. They wanted to break him, yes. But sometimes being beaten and standing again teaches more than winning a fight ever will. He needed to learn he could survive. You stole that from him.

I grind my teeth, pressing harder at the bars as the scene fades.

The bars flicker, and the Presence pulls me sideways, not forward, not back, just… inward. Shadows fold until I see it again: Jack. Tied to the chair, eyes wet, begging. Michael had the knife ready. Lucian was spitting fire. Jace was begging for mercy. And me? I was clawing at the wheel, laughing, ready to carve the truth out of him.

The Presence speaks steady. If you had taken control then, Amelia would've lost her father. Jack would've died on your blade, and the tracker would still be buried in his neck. You would've silenced answers instead of finding them.

My hands clench. He's right, and it burns.

The shadows bend again. The bike roars under me, night air cutting sharp across skin. Oldsmobile tailing close. Two riders creeping in. I remember the hunger in my teeth, the need to rip them apart with my hands instead of letting the city do the work. Michael held the wheel. He let traffic, metal, and bad timing do the bleeding.

Here, you were not needed. *The Presence says it calm.* Your way would've been louder. Messier. Bodies in the street, blood on the bike. The job was to escape, not to paint the pavement red.

The shadows fade, bars humming around me again. My chest heaves, rage and pride knotted together. The Presence does not move. He never does.

Not every moment belongs to the storm, *he says.* But when the storm comes, it must come full.

The bars shimmer again, and the Presence drags me sideways. A different night. Madison in the bar for the first time. Michael drinking, Lucian prowling, Jace already drunk. A drunk had put his hands on her. I remember surging up, ready to cave the man's skull against the counter. Lucian slipped in instead, cold and precise, handled it with two moves. No storm needed. Just control.

The Presence speaks calm. Not every insult deserves fire. Sometimes precision cuts deeper than rage.

The air changes again. Dawn. Madison's pier, cold air biting. Jace's heart hammering. She laughed for the first time in weeks, and it tore at me. Laughter is fragile. It doesn't last. I wanted out, to break the world before it could take that sound away from her. Instead, Jace let her breathe. Ten more minutes of peace, stolen back from the world.

Not every shadow must be met with fire. *The Presence says it without judgment.*

The memory shatters to another. Puerto Rico. Gunfire thick, too many angles. Marco's men pressing hard. Michael's hand shook, Jace screamed in the dark. That was me, ripping forward, breaking the tide. Scar tissue on Marco's throat remembers my grip even now.

Here, you were needed. Without you, there would have been no tomorrow.

The bars snap back into place, humming like they've been waiting for me to break. My chest heaves. My fists bleed. I slam them into the iron again and again, shadows sparking with each strike.

Then why do I exist at all if I'm not meant to burn every enemy to ash?!

The Presence does not flinch. His voice is steady, heavier than chains, softer than stone worn smooth by rivers. Because storms that never end do not protect. They destroy.

My fists split open, knuckles raw against bars that don't give. Blood runs, but it doesn't fall. It hisses, disappears, swallowed by the shadow. Even my rage gets devoured here.

I EXIST TO DESTROY. *My roar shakes the cage, rattles inside the skulls of the others though they can't hear it. My voice should level cities, should turn bone to powder. Here, it's swallowed by silence.*

The Presence does not move. The weight of him presses closer, not crushing, not punishing, simply there. Unflinching.

Let me out! *I snarl, throat raw.* Let me take the wheel and I'll tear Marco to ribbons. I'll put his men in the dirt, feed their bones to the street. I'll get her back!

The Presence's reply is not louder than me. It doesn't need to be. It slides into the silence after my rage like a blade into flesh.
And then what? What will be left of her when you arrive dripping in their blood?

The question cuts deeper than chains. My hands shake on the bars. I slam my head against them once, twice, until the world bursts white behind my eyes.

Better a storm than a corpse! *I bellow.* Better fire than silence!

The bars hum, resonant, unbroken. The Presence is steady as ever, a mountain unmoved by the storm clawing at its roots.
Storms pass. Silence holds. You cannot protect by devouring what you were made to guard.

I howl, a sound that would rip lungs in half outside this cage. Here it breaks useless against the iron shadows. My chest heaves. My throat tears. And still… the Presence does not move.

At last, my arms fall heavy to my sides. Breath ragged. Blood on my lips from biting too hard. I slump against the bars, forehead pressed to iron that isn't iron. The rage still burns, but it eats me instead of the world.

The Presence does not gloat. Does not mock. He only speaks, low and patient. There will come a time when you are the only answer left. When restraint will not save them. That is when the gate opens.

I hate the calm in his voice more than any chain.

I stay pressed against the bars, chest heaving, rage blistering in my veins with nowhere to go. The fire chews at me from the inside, hungry for bone, for blood, for release. The Presence doesn't answer my silence. He lets me drown in it. Patient. Always patient.

Tell me, storm… how would you feel if they were gone?

The words slam harder than chains. My head jerks up, eyes wide, fire clawing higher in my chest.

Gone? *I snarl, voice low, guttural.* They won't be gone. I won't let them—

If Michael falters. If Jace breaks. If Lucian bleeds out his last joke. If Madison's fire is smothered. If Z's screens go dark. If one day… they are no more.

The bars hum with his words, like the cage itself carries them.

What would you be then? Protector with nothing left to guard. Rage with no one to shield.

My stomach knots, fury twisting into something I don't recognize. Not fear. Not grief. Something worse: emptiness. The thought gnaws at me, hollowing out the fire in my chest until it sputters against the question I can't kill.

I press my forehead to the shadows, eyes squeezed shut, breath ragged. The fire rages still—but now, for the first time, there's ash in it.

If they're gone… then I burn the world. I tear it down to ash, brick by brick, until nothing stands. If I can't protect them, I'll avenge them. That's what I am. That's what I'll always be.

The words echo, harsh, final. My voice shakes the cage, but the Presence doesn't move. He never does. Instead, he lets the silence settle, heavier than before.

Then, his voice comes low. Steady. Cutting deeper.

And if you were gone too? What if Michael's mind is dust. Jace's courage bled away. Lucian's tongue stilled. Madison's spark snuffed out. Z's light black. And you, storm… you too. No rage. No wheel. No fire. Nothing.

The bars vibrate with his words. The weight of them crushes down until my snarl falters. My throat dries. For a moment, the cage is silent except for my own breath, too loud, too uneven.

If… if we're all gone— *I start, but the fire stutters halfway through. My grip on the bars slips, palms raw, blood slick.*

The Presence does not flinch. His voice is calm, as if the question has always been waiting.

Then what are you? *He asks.*

The fire in me thrashes, desperate to answer, but for the first time… it doesn't know how. The silence presses in, heavier than rage, heavier than chains.

Finally, I force the words out, raw, jagged.

Why… why the hell would you even ask me that?

He does not shift. Does not raise his voice. His reply comes low, calm, steady as stone weathered smooth by rivers.

Just curious, is all.

Ashes in My Mouth

Madison

The room still smelled like blood. My blood. It clung to the concrete, copper sharp under the mildew and sweat, thick enough I could taste it every time I drew a breath. My jaw ached. One eye swelled shut, pulsing in time with my heartbeat. The straps had dug so deep into my wrists they'd left raw grooves that burned worse than the fists.

The guards had left minutes ago. I could still hear their boots echoing down the corridor, fading under the low hum of the compound. Marco hadn't needed to stay. He knew the echo of him was enough.

I let my head sag forward, strands of hair sticking to the blood drying on my cheek. My throat tasted like ash when I whispered to the empty room.

"Michael…"

I hated myself for it. For even thinking his name. For waiting like he was a prayer when I knew better. Hope was a weakness Marco loved carving out of me. He always came back for it first. And still… my chest ached with the thought of him. Not just Michael. All of them. The pieces of him I'd glimpsed. The storm behind his eyes. The voice that had warned me once to run. The others who bled and laughed and planned in the same body.

And the one Marco didn't even understand. The one he should fear most.

I lifted my head slowly, ignoring the fire down my neck, ignoring the room still swaying from the last hit. The straps groaned as I flexed against them. I wasn't breaking free, but the motion reminded me I was still here. Still breathing. That counted for something.

"Marco thinks he owns me. Marco thinks he owns the brooch. Marco thinks he's already won."

I smiled, teeth red, the kind of smile he hated. Because no matter how deep he cut, he couldn't cut out the one truth I carried like armor.

"He's coming," I whispered. "And not just Michael."

The words burned in my throat, but they gave me strength, enough to lift my head when I heard the door's lock grind open again. Boots on concrete. Slower this time. Measured. Marco didn't rush. He never had to.

Two guards stepped in first, faces blank, rifles hanging low but ready. Then Marco appeared behind them, smoothing his cufflinks like this was just another meeting. His cologne cut through the blood and mildew, sharp enough to make my stomach twist.

He waved the guards off with a flick of his hand. They stayed by the door. He wanted them close enough to watch, far enough that I had no illusion of privacy.

Marco crouched low in front of me, elbows resting casually on his knees, eyes level with mine. The smile he wore wasn't warm, wasn't cruel—it was the mask he liked best, the one that said he already knew the ending.

"You're still fighting," he said quietly, almost admiring. "It's a shame, really. You could have had a softer life if you'd just learned to obey."

My jaw ached with every word, but I forced my eyes to lock on his. "Obeying isn't living. And I'll never live on my knees for you."

Marco chuckled, low in his throat, but there was no humor in it. He reached out, fingers brushing my jaw the way someone might test glass for cracks.

"One day, Madison," he said, voice still calm, "you'll learn that even the hardest glass shatters when struck enough times in the right place."

I flinched at his touch but forced the smile back onto my bloodied lips. "Then keep swinging. You'll die before you find the spot."

His eyes narrowed at that, the faintest crack in the mask. Marco straightened slowly, tugging his cuffs back into place like my words had scuffed him.

"You always had that mouth," he said, voice sharpening. "Sharp enough to cut yourself with. You think it makes you strong? No. It just makes you bleed faster."

He circled behind me, slow and deliberate, his presence heavy on my shoulders. His breath brushed my ear when he spoke again.

"And you keep talking about Michael, like he's some savior on his way. You don't understand, he's already mine. My men brought him in before the sun came up."

My chest tightened, but I forced my eyes forward, jaw clenched against the straps.

"You're lying."

Marco's chuckle was low, steady, too calm to dismiss. He leaned close, close enough that I could feel the heat of his words.

"Believe what you want. But as we speak, your so-called protector is in a darker room than this one, with heavier chains. He's no different than you. He'll beg just the same."

I shook my head, forcing the bloodied smile back to my lips. "No. He'll burn through you before he begs."

The mask cracked again, anger flashing hot and raw in his eyes. He slammed his palm against the chair's back, the sound exploding through the room.

"Careful, Madison," he hissed. "Keep pushing, and I'll remind you exactly how small you are in this house."

The words should have slid past me like every other threat, but they didn't. They stuck, heavy, because of what came before them.

Michael.

I swallowed hard, my throat raw. "If you have him… let him go. He has nothing to do with this. He doesn't know about the brooch, about—about any of it. He's just…"

I bit down before the words could keep tumbling out, but it was too late. Marco's eyes sharpened at the crack in my voice. He leaned closer, smiling like he'd just heard the first true thing all night.

"Just what?" he pressed. "What is he to you, Madison? Protector? Lover? Or something else?"

My chest rose and fell too fast. Fear clawed at me, tripping over defiance. I wanted to rip the words back, but they spilled anyway.

"He's not alone," I snapped. "You think it's only Michael, but you don't understand. There are others…"

I froze, teeth grinding shut, but the damage was done. His expression flickered with interest, the kind of cold curiosity I knew too well.

"Others," Marco repeated softly, savoring the word. "How many? Who are they?"

I shook my head hard. "You don't know what you're talking about."

But he didn't move, didn't lash out. He just smiled wider, patient, like a predator who had all night.

"Oh, I think I do," he murmured. "You just gave me more than I had a minute ago."

He straightened slowly, pacing in front of me, eyes locked on mine like I was a puzzle he'd just found a missing piece for.

"Others," he repeated. "How many, Madison? Who are they? Friends? Men you ran to when you left me? Or are they here, hiding in that broken little head of yours right alongside him?"

I bit down until I tasted blood, refusing to answer.

His patience cracked. He leaned in, his hand snapping up to grip my face, fingers digging into my bruised jaw until pain spiked through my skull.

"Tell me!" he snarled, squeezing harder. "Who are they? How many are there? What are their names?"

My eyes watered, but I forced them to stay locked on his. "You'll never understand."

His grip tightened, thumb pressing cruelly into the swelling at my cheekbone. "Then make me understand! Say it! Say their names!"

I shook my head as much as his hand allowed, every muscle trembling, my voice ragged but steady. "No."

Marco's face darkened, his mask slipping. For the first time, he looked less like the calm man in control and more like the violent truth underneath. He shook me once, hard enough that my teeth clacked together.

"You think I won't break you?" he hissed. "You think silence will save them? Nothing will. Not Michael. Not these 'others.' Not you."

I spit blood against his hand. "Then keep trying."

His jaw flexed, rage burning hot in his eyes. He let go with a sharp shove, like touching me any longer might make him lose control. He stood, smoothing his cuffs again, trying to paste the mask back over the fury that had slipped.

Marco stayed where he was, looming over me, adjusting his cuffs like he hadn't just lost control a second ago. His eyes, though, sharp, hungry, never left mine.

"You slipped, Madison," he said quietly. "And slips mean truth. You said 'others.' Not once. Twice. Who are they?

What do they call themselves when they crawl out from
behind his face?"

I shook my head, lips pressed tight.

He smirked. "Do they have names? Do they have different
voices? Do they whisper to you at night when you're in his
bed? Tell me, which one touched you? Which one made
you laugh?"

My stomach twisted, but I didn't give him the satisfaction
of looking away. "You wouldn't understand."

"Oh, I understand more than you think." His hand shot
out again, gripping my chin, forcing my head to tilt back
until my neck screamed. "He's dangerous, isn't he? That's
why you ran to him. Because you saw the same thing I did.
The man who scarred me isn't the one who smiles at you.
It wasn't Michael that night. It was one of them."

His fingers dug deeper, until tears welled hot in my eyes. I
bit down a sob.

"Who was it?" he demanded. "Which one gave me this
scar?" He tilted his head, the faint white line across his
throat catching in the overhead light. His voice dropped,
low and venomous. "Was it the one you whisper about in
your sleep?"

I tried to turn away, but his grip held me like iron. "I don't
know what you're talking about."

"Yes, you do." His smile was thin, cruel. "The way you just
flinched told me everything. There's one that terrifies even
you. Isn't there?"

I glared at him through my one good eye. "He terrifies everyone."

Marco laughed then, a short, sharp bark that sent a chill crawling up my spine. "Good. That means he bleeds like the rest of you. And when I find him, I'll put him down the same way I'll put Michael down. One bullet. One cut. And it's finished."

"You can't kill what you don't understand," I spat, voice shaking.

He leaned closer, his breath hot on my face. "Then make me understand. Tell me about them. Tell me who else is hiding behind that man's eyes."

I refused to answer, jaw tight, breathing sharp.

"Nothing?" Marco sneered. "Then I'll tell you what I think. I think you're protecting him. Protecting them. Maybe you even love one of them more than you love Michael. Maybe that's why you won't speak."

"That's not true," I snapped before I could stop myself.

His grin widened instantly. "Ah. So, I'm right."

I froze, heart hammering in my chest.

"You see? You betray yourself without me even touching you. That's the problem, Madison. You've always been too easy to read. And now I know, there's more than one man inside that head you cling to. Which means more weaknesses. More ways to break him. And more ways to break you."

I swallowed back bile, forcing the words out through clenched teeth. "You'll never get to them."

"Oh, I will," he said calmly. "Because you'll bring them to me. Maybe not with words. But with every look, every twitch, every time I mention Michael's name. You've already started."

His voice dropped into a whisper, cruel and intimate. "And when I cut one of them down, I'll make you watch. I'll make you see the pieces of him disappear until there's nothing left but a hollow shell. And then I'll put you back where you belong, at my side."

I yanked against the straps hard enough to tear my wrists open again. "Never."

Marco stood back, smoothing his shirt, expression controlled once more. "Never is a long time, Madison. We'll see how long it lasts when you're thirsty, starving, and alone with your thoughts."

He turned halfway toward the door, then stopped, glancing back over his shoulder. His eyes locked onto mine, cold and steady.

"And remember, Michael's already in my hands. You'll both break. The only question is which one of you goes first."

Marco didn't move toward the door after all. He stepped back in front of me, crouching again, elbows balanced on his knees, face inches from mine. His tone softened, not with kindness but with the same edge he used on his men before making an example out of them.

"You know what the real tragedy is, Madison?" he said. "It isn't that you betrayed me. It isn't even that you ran. It's that you don't know him. Not really. You've seen pieces, shadows, and you're clinging to them like they're whole men."

My throat tightened. "I know more than you ever will."

"Do you?" His brows lifted, like I'd just proven his point. "Tell me which one is real. Michael? Jace? Whoever else is rattling around in there? You talk about them like they're separate, but they all wear the same skin. Do you even know which one held you at night? Do you even know who kissed you?"

Heat flared in my face, but I stayed silent.

He chuckled darkly. "You don't. That's the truth. And when I cut them down one by one, you won't even know which man you lost. That's what you've tied yourself to, a ghost with too many faces. Pathetic."

I clenched my fists against the straps, nails digging into open wounds until I felt the sting. He wanted me to doubt. To unravel. I couldn't let him.

"You don't understand him," I said, voice steady even though my insides shook. "He's more than you could ever imagine."

Marco's smile widened. "Then explain it. Help me understand."

I stayed silent.

"Nothing?" His hand snapped out, seizing my jaw again, squeezing until stars burst behind my eyes. "You're protecting him because you're afraid, Madison. Afraid of what he really is. Afraid of what he'll do to you when he's finished playing hero. Maybe that's why you ran from me, to trade one monster for another."

The words cut deeper than his grip. For a heartbeat, doubt wormed its way in, ugly and sharp. Michael wasn't just Michael. He was Jace. He was Lucian. And somewhere, caged but never gone, was HIM. Not a shadow. Not a whisper. I had spoken to him. I had touched him. I had seen the hunger in his eyes and laid a hand on his cheek when his rage threatened to consume everything. He had let me close when no one else dared.

That's why he terrified me. Because I knew exactly what lived in him, and exactly what it would do to the world if the bars ever broke.

But fear didn't mean surrender.

I forced a smile through the pain, blood slick on my teeth. "The difference is, he terrifies you more."

Marco's nostrils flared. He shook me once, hard, before releasing my face with a shove. He stood, rolling his shoulders, trying to calm himself again but not quite succeeding.

"Let's pretend you're right," he said, pacing slowly. "Let's say there are… others. He can't keep them hidden forever. Every slip of his tongue, every twitch of his eye, his secrets bleed, just like you bled for me tonight. And when they do, I'll be waiting. I'll strip them away, one by one. And when there's nothing left, I'll put what's left of him at your feet. We'll see if you smile then."

I sucked in a sharp breath, shaking my head. "You'll never break him."

"Maybe not," Marco allowed. "But I can break you. And you, Madison, you're easier. You've always been easier."

He stopped in front of me again, crouching low so his eyes met mine. His voice softened to a whisper. "Michael will scream before the end. Do you want to know why? Not because of me. Because of you. Because he'll hear you crying in the next room, and he'll know it's his fault."

I flinched, my throat clenching against a sob I refused to let out. Marco saw it anyway. His smile returned, cruel and thin.

"Ah. There it is. The truth. You can deny it all you want, but you just showed me exactly where to press."

He stood and smoothed his shirt like we'd just had a civil conversation. He glanced at the guards by the door, his mask firmly back in place. "No food. No water. She can sit with her thoughts until tonight. We'll see how much her silence is worth when she's parched and begging."

The guards nodded. Marco looked back at me one last time, eyes steady, voice calm. "Remember Madison, you told me about them. Not me. You. And I never waste a gift."

He left with the same slow, measured steps he'd come in with, leaving me strapped down, bloodied, shaking, but not broken. Not yet.

Watching the Wires

Michael

Dawn bled through the cracks in the safe house shutters, thin lines of light slicing across the table where the map still lay scattered with grease-stained wrappers. The generator coughed once, steadying into its low hum.

Z finally stirred against me, muttering something incoherent before rolling off the cot with a groan. "Coffee," she mumbled, snatching Conner's cup without asking.

Conner grunted from his post at the door but didn't stop her. His eyes hadn't left the tree line since he sat down. Rifle loose in his lap, finger never far from the trigger. "You'll need more than caffeine," he said flat. "Dockside's alive already. Marco's men are tightening the screws."

I pushed myself upright, stretching the stiffness from my shoulders. "Rumors?"

"More than rumors." Conner flicked his chin toward the window. "Checkpoints doubled overnight. Locals say he's buying silence with food and cash. He's spooked. He knows someone's here." His eyes cut to me, sharp. "He knows it's you."

Z set the cup down, rubbing her temples as she pulled her laptop closer. "Good. Let him sweat. Fear makes people sloppy."

Lucian hummed inside, amused. *I like her. She thinks like us.* Jace's voice steadied against the edge of my thoughts. *Or she thinks like HIM. Careful, Michael.*

I ignored them both, leaning over the map again. The northern pier still circled in ink, the seam waiting. "We need eyes on the ground. Patterns. Movement. Weak points Marco doesn't even know he's showing."

Conner shifted in his chair. "You want recon."

"Yes."

He stood, slinging the rifle over his shoulder. "Then we move before the city's fully awake. Less eyes. Less noise."

Z stretched, hoodie sliding up one shoulder, and dug her phone out from the desk clutter. "Two minutes," she muttered, already dialing.

Conner frowned. "Now?"

"Yeah, now." She shot him a look sharp enough to cut. "You don't own every second of my time."

She paced to the corner, back turned, voice dropping softer than I'd heard in days. "Hey, babe. …Yeah, I'm fine. No, I slept. Sort of." A pause, then a laugh low enough to almost sound foreign in this room. "You worry too much. …I'll be careful. Promise."

Lucian stirred in the back of my head, smirking. *Cute. Hacker queen gets all soft.*

Jace cut him off, steady. *Leave her be. Everyone needs someone. Even us.*

I kept my face blank, but my ears caught every word. She wasn't lying. Not exactly. But she wasn't telling her girl the kind of work this was either. Some truths couldn't be softened.

The call ended quickly. Z shoved the phone back in her pocket and grabbed her laptop. The softness was gone, her smirk sliding back into place. "Alright. Let's go see what Marco's hiding."

Conner muttered, "About time." He checked his rifle strap and moved for the door.

I pulled on my jacket, the brooch heavy in my pocket. "No noise today. Just eyes. We see where the seams are."

We slipped out into the morning. Damp heat wrapped around us like a blanket, jungle steam mixing with the salt off the coast. Barceloneta was already alive—vendors setting up, shutters clanging, stray dogs nosing through trash. Marco's men stood out. Too rigid. Eyes always scanning.

Conner led steadily, Z drifted just behind with her screen tilted low, pulling signals from the air as we walked. I kept my eyes on the alleys, the rooftops, the places where rifles could gleam.

Barceloneta hadn't forgotten me. The air carried it. The tension sat like static across the back of my neck.

The streets narrowed as we pushed closer to the docks. Concrete sagged into cracked pavement, laundry lines drooped low between rust-eaten balconies, and the stink of fish and diesel clung to everything. The salt in the air bit at the back of my throat, sharp enough to remind me I'd been here before. Barceloneta never forgot.

Conner walked point, rifle low, steady like he'd mapped every corner. Z hung a step behind him, laptop tilted in her hands, her fingers twitching over keys like she was pulling invisible threads from the air. To anyone else, we looked like a soldier, a hacker, and a shadow trailing behind. To me, it felt like the edge of a knife pressing closer to skin.

Everywhere I looked, Marco's men stuck out. Posture too rigid. Eyes too sharp. Locals kept their heads down, carrying crates or tugging shutters open, but the guards? They scanned. Always scanning. Checkpoints weren't random, they were rhythm.

The static crawled over my neck. Too many eyes. Too many angles. My instincts wanted to snap forward, calculate, react, tear down anything that moved wrong. My pulse hitched, steady but hard. I felt the table shift inside, the pressure building.

Let me, Jace's voice said, calm but firm. *This part's mine.*

My jaw clenched. My eyes swept the rooftops again, the alleys, the crates stacked high where rifles might be hidden.

Observation's yours, I admitted finally. *Just don't lose the mask.*

I let him.

The shift was subtle, just a tightening in my chest, a sharpening of the edges around me. The world slowed into rhythm. Boots hitting pavement in staggered counts. Rifles lifting and dropping in predictable arcs. Guards weren't just men anymore—they were moving pieces in a pattern I could read.

(Jace)

The shift settled. My chest loosened, my focus sharpened. Noise faded into rhythm. That's always how it felt when I stepped forward—like the world had been cluttered until I straightened it out.

Two guards by the east checkpoint. Their rifles weren't cradled like men standing easy, they were braced. Watching. Four more by the southern crates, pretending to unload cargo but keeping their eyes on every passerby. And there—a sniper posted on a mid-building balcony.

His scope drifted. Lazy. Tired. The kind of mistake you only caught if you watched long enough.

"Two east, four south, one above. Mid-balcony," I murmured, keeping my voice even. "Sniper's slacking."

Conner flicked his eyes back at me, quick and sharp. He didn't say anything, just shifted his route like he trusted it.

Z glanced sideways at me, smirk tugging at her mouth. "See? Always sharper when it's quiet."

I kept my stride steady, jaw locked, playing Michael. To Conner, that's all I could be—scarred soldier, strategist, nothing more.

Inside, Lucian lounged, voice dripping with amusement. *Boy Scout's got the reins. Don't trip, hero.*

Michael's voice cut in firm. *Mask stays on. Conner can't know.*

I didn't answer. I just kept scanning. The world was a map in motion. Every turn of a rifle, every step of a boot, every breath misting in the morning air—patterns, all of it.

"Checkpoint rotates south in ninety seconds," I muttered. "Blind spot between the pier and southern unit. That's our gap."

Conner's jaw flexed, but he moved like he believed me. Z adjusted her bag higher, her screen glowing faint against her hoodie. "Then let's not waste it."

The city didn't breathe the way New York did. It was slower, heavier, like the air itself was dragging. That made it easier for me—movements stood out sharper. Even the guards thought they blended into the hum of Barceloneta, but I saw every seam.

We cut along the edge of the market, where fishmongers were already stacking crates in sloppy towers. Between them, I caught the flash of a pistol grip tucked into the waistband of a man pretending to barter. Cartel eyes, not a customer.

"Plainclothes," I muttered, low. "Two o'clock, stalling near the stall with the blue tarp. He's not shopping."

Conner didn't look. Didn't need to. His pace shifted, subtle, sliding us just wide enough that the man lost his angle.

Z smirked, her eyes flicking over her screen. "And here I thought you were just muscle."

I didn't answer. Couldn't. Michael would've said something sharp back, but I kept my mouth shut. Mask on.

We crossed toward the southern road. Guards rotated in twos there, rifles hanging casual, but their eyes stayed on anyone too still. Timing mattered. One group stepped off, boots echoing against the cracked pavement. The replacement squad was late—just by seconds, but I caught it.

"There," I said under my breath. "Southern rotation drags its feet. Forty seconds exposed before the relief comes in."

"Forty seconds isn't much," Conner muttered.

"It's enough," I said.

Lucian's laugh slid through the back of my head. *You always were the little stopwatch, weren't you?*

I ignored him.

We hugged the shadow of a warehouse, salt-stained walls rising tall, broken glass crunching under Conner's boots. I scanned the rooftops again. One sniper I'd already clocked, scope drifting. But two more were nested—one prone near the north pier crane, another crouched behind a broken billboard. Their rifles didn't sweep. They stayed locked on choke points.

"Three snipers," I said quietly. "One lazy, two fixed. They're funneling, forcing approaches."

Conner's jaw flexed. "Means they're expecting movement."

"They're expecting noise," I corrected. "We don't give them any."

The docks stretched open now, floodlights dimmed in the morning haze but still humming. Cargo containers stacked three high, red and blue, arranged like a maze. Too neat. Too deliberate. And scattered in between, men in pairs with rifles, pretending to be dockhands. They weren't unloading, weren't working—they were waiting.

"Outer ring's a trap," I said. "Too many pretending. If we walk into that, we're dead before the gate."

Z tilted her laptop just enough to flash lines of scrolling code. "Signal confirms it. Half their radios are on one channel, half on another. Two nets. Inner ring and outer. They're talking like they don't trust each other."

I scanned again, watching the rhythm of their steps, the tension in their shoulders. She was right. They weren't one machine—they were two halves stitched together. That seam mattered.

"Marco's overextended," I muttered. "He doubled the guard but split their loyalty. Some are real cartel, the rest are bought muscle. That means nerves. Weak discipline. Easy to spook."

Z smirked faintly. "So, we spook them first?"

"Not yet," I said.

We pushed deeper, sticking to the alleys. The closer we got, the more I saw—the checkpoint logs, the way crates were left as false cover, the crates with fresh paint that weren't marked at all. I tapped Conner's shoulder and nodded toward them.

"Explosives," I said flat. "Unmarked, new paint. Too clean. That's their fail-safe if the pier gets overrun."

Conner cursed under his breath. "So, Marco's willing to burn his own product before letting it fall."

I nodded.

My focus sharpened harder, my heart matching the rhythm of boots and rifles. Every step added to the map in my head. Rotations. Blind spots. Weak points. By the time we curved back toward the safer streets, I could see it all like ink etched under my skin.

"We've got it," I whispered. "The whole board."

We cut back through the alleys, looping toward the safer streets. The map in my head was complete now— rotations, blind spots, pressure points. We had enough.

That's when I heard it.

Boots. Not the slow rhythm of a patrol shift. Fast. Coming closer.

I froze, hand shooting out to halt Z and Conner. Conner's brow furrowed, but he stilled instantly. Z's eyes darted from her screen to the corner ahead.

Two men rounded it first, rifles slung but eyes sharp. Another pair followed, one already talking low into a radio. A patrol, but too close, too quick. They weren't supposed to sweep this sector for another five minutes.

Michael stirred hard inside me. *Mask on, Jace. If they clock us, we drop them fast.*

No, I thought back. *Not here. Too loud. We don't win this with noise.*

Lucian's voice was lazy, sharp around the edges. *Then smile, Boy Scout. Play it cool.*

My pulse didn't change. My stride did. I pushed forward before Conner could react, shoulders loose, posture steady—the way Michael walked when he wanted the world to believe he belonged anywhere.

The guards' eyes swept over us. One lingered too long, suspicion flickering. His hand shifted toward his rifle strap.

"Morning," I said flat, just loud enough. My Spanish wasn't perfect, but I let the confidence do the work. "Patrol's running fast today."

It wasn't a question. It was a statement, like I was meant to be here, like I had the authority to notice.

The man stiffened, glanced at the one with the radio. For a second the air tightened like a noose. Then the leader grunted, muttered something sharp about "rotation changes," and waved them on.

They passed. Boots fading. Radios crackling low until the sound bled back into the buzz of the city.

I exhaled once through my nose, forcing my hands to stay loose at my sides.

Z smirked faintly, voice low. "Nice save, old man."

Conner's eyes cut at me, sharp, suspicious, but he didn't say anything.

We didn't speak until we'd cleared three more blocks and slipped back into the quiet edges of Barceloneta. Conner led us through the jungle's fringe, doubling back twice to make sure no tails followed. Only when the safe house door shut behind us did I let the breath I'd been holding go.

The generator hummed. The smell of cold fried chicken lingered. Same four walls, but now I carried a whole city under my skin.

I moved straight to the table, dragging the map closer. My hand closed around the pencil stub Z had left, and I started sketching. Arcs for guard rotations. Circles for snipers. Crosshatches for choke points.

"Three snipers," I said. "One mid-balcony, lazy. Two fixed: crane north pier, billboard south face. They funnel movement through the main dock lanes. Southern rotation lags forty seconds. That's the seam."

Lines cut the paper as I marked them.

"Outer rings stacked with fake dockhands. Pretending to unload, but their rifles give them away. That's the trap. Walk into it, and we're boxed. Inner ring's cartel loyal. Outer's hired muscle. Two nets. Two chains of command."

Z leaned over my shoulder, nodding, her smirk fading as the picture filled. "That's why the radios split."

"Yeah," I said. "And those crates with fresh paint by the south wall? Not cargo. Explosives. Marco would rather burn his own product than risk a breach."

Conner stood across the table, arms folded, eyes narrowing at the map. "You saw all that."

"Yeah."

He didn't say anything else, but I caught the twitch of his jaw, the way his eyes lingered on me like he was trying to measure the man he was looking at. I held the stare, kept the mask. Michael's mask.

The silence stretched until Z broke it. "Then we know the board."

I set the pencil down, the map scarred with new lines. "We know the board," I echoed. "Next step is how to break it."

No one argued.

The generator coughed once, steadying. Outside, the jungle buzzed like it was listening. I leaned back, palms flat against the table, letting the weight of the map settle over all of us.

"We got enough for tonight," I said. "Tomorrow is what worries me."

Z leaned back in her chair, arms crossed, eyes steady on mine. "Tomorrow, we test it. Don't oversleep."

Dry Run

Jace

Morning hit thick and slow. Conner brewed coffee strong enough to clean engine parts. Z ate cold chicken over her keyboard.

"We're not storming," I said. "We're touching the fence and walking away. Three goals: pull a radio off the outer ring, clone a badge, map one interior hallway on the inner net. If we do more, we did too much."

Conner nodded once. "I've got a man at the fish market. He won't love it, but he'll look the other way."

Z slid a pouch across the table. "Badge skimmer, short-range. Thirty seconds pressed to the plastic. And a mic that lives on their channel for twelve hours. Plant it, walk."

Michael was quiet inside, listening. Lucian yawned like a cat that smelled a fight and didn't care yet. I laced my boots tighter and tried not to think about Madison's wrists.

We moved at shift change. Same route as yesterday, different pace. Conner took us through a side street where laundry lines sagged low enough to hide a rifle. Z fell in behind me, hoodie up, a tourist who'd made a bad turn.

The outer pier was all noise—crates, yelling, diesel. That worked in our favor. Noise meant cover.

First pull was the radio.

I picked a dockhand with cartel shoulders and a clean vest. He leaned to light a cigarette; I stepped into him like I belonged there, bumped an apology in Spanish, palmed the spare unit from his belt as Z coughed loud to cover the click. He checked his pocket, found his lighter, forgot the rest.

We were gone in three steps.

"Easy," Z murmured.

"Next," I said.

The badge would be harder. You can't fake heat. You have to look like you work here or like you own the place. I chose work.

We drifted toward the southern checkpoint where the lag lived. A supervisor with a clipboard ran his mouth to two guards. His badge swung free.

Z peeled off to a vendor cart and "accidentally" knocked a tray of plastic spoons into his path. He swore, bent to help, I knelt opposite, pressed the skimmer behind the badge lanyard as my other hand scooped spoons. Thirty seconds feels like a minute when your ribs are open to a rifle barrel.

The skimmer buzzed once in my palm. Copy made.

"Gracias," I said, deadpan.

He didn't look at me. Perfect.

Conner's voice brushed low. "Eyes," he warned.

Two plainclothes watched too long from the shade of a container stack. I guided us into a row of pallets like we were cutting through for shade. Z trailed a half step, already palming the mic.

We reached a bolt-upright floodlight pole near the inner gate. Crews changed there. Radios clipped to belts, chatter high. Z knelt to "tie a shoe," peeled a magnet backer off the mic, slapped it to the pole base, and snapped her gum.

"Planted," she breathed.

"Walk," I said.

We almost made it clean.

A kid—couldn't be more than twenty—stepped out of a shadow with a clipboard and a new badge on a fresh lanyard. He had the keyed-up energy of someone trying very hard to look official. He picked the wrong people to stop.

"Credentials," he said, chin up.

Conner shifted to block his sightline to Z. I gave the kid the look men give when they don't plan to be delayed.

"Supervisor wanted the manifest records," I said, bored. "Now he's busting my ass about the crane schedule."

The kid's eyes flicked to the crane, back to my face, then to Conner's rifle sling. Sweat beaded. He didn't know if we were above him or beneath him, only that we were in a hurry. He swallowed and stepped aside.

We flowed through and out the south edge like water.

Three blocks later, tucked inside a noise of scooters and a panadería line, Z slid the radio into her bag and set the skimmer on my palm like it was an egg.

"Good," she said, not smiling. "Now we see if your thirty seconds was thirty."

Back at the safe house, the generator grumbled. Z set the radio on the table, cracked it open, soldering iron already hot. Conner locked the door and did a perimeter sweep without being asked.

I dumped the skimmer's guts into her laptop. A badge number popped. Then a name: Álvarez, L. Level 2 access.

"Gate and admin doors," Z said, scanning the hex like sheet music. "Not inner wing. But it gets us further than the yard."

"Good enough for today," I said.

Conner pulled a folded map he'd hand-drawn years ago and dropped it next to the radio. "There's a service corridor behind the admin wing. When they upgraded cameras, they skipped the duct above the old archive room. Dust and rats. No lens."

I traced it with a finger. "That puts us one wall off the inner hallway."

Z clipped the radio back together. "If the mic sticks, we'll know when they rotate the inner wing medical. They always run a water run after beatings. Biohazard rules. "We get water, towels, stretchers' on the net—we follow it to her." Silence landed hard.

Michael pushed forward enough to be a presence. I didn't fight him. He didn't take control, just leaned cold against my shoulder.

"Test the mic," I said.

Z flicked a switch. Static hissed, then voices layered in— outer ring chatter, forklift swears, a supervisor chewing someone out about pallets. She twisted the dial. Another channel bled in, tighter discipline, different cadence.

"…shift change in corridor two…"

"Hold," Z said, hand up.

A beat. "—infirmary requests additional towels. Blood on a chair. Bring water. Now."

My stomach turned to stone. Conner's jaw locked. Michael's presence sharpened like a blade cooling in water.

"She's alive," I said, because the alternative wasn't an option I'd say out loud.

Z didn't look up. "We're not moving today," she said. "We use this to learn the timing. We confirm the route. We build the jump with what we have, not what we want."

Lucian finally spoke low. *We're still breathing because the kid notices clocks.*

I exhaled through my nose. "We're still not enough men for a grab in the inner wing with just Level 2."

Conner nodded once. "Then we get Level 3."

"How?" Z asked.

"Maintenance," I said. "They touch everything. They hate everyone. And their cards open the wrong doors because some admin never toggled a checkbox."

Z's mouth twitched. "So, we fish a janitor."

"Tonight, we don't fish anyone," I said. "We listen. We map the water run twice. If it repeats, we know the cart route. Tomorrow we take the cart."

Conner tapped the map where the service corridor hit a dead space. "You'll need a place to stash what you steal for one hour without a patrol sniffing it."

"Duct above archive," I said. "You already gave it to me."

He grunted. That passed for approval.

The radio cracked again.

"—bring a stretcher to aisle four—"

Z wrote fast. "Time stamp."

We ran the sequence three more times before midday. Same phrases, different orders, same window: inner wing calls towels and water eight minutes after a shift change. Stretcher seven minutes after that. The cart route skirted the admin hallway every time.

Z slid the paper to me. "That's your hole."

Michael pressed harder at the back of my skull. I let the pressure sit. He'd get the wheel when it was time to drive into a wall. This wasn't that.

"Conner," I said, "you still have uniforms?"

"Two," he said. "One fits you, one almost fits me. Z runs comms. She doesn't go inside."

Z opened her mouth.

"Not this pass," I said, and didn't soften it.

She watched me, then flicked a look to the radio and back. "Fine. But I build your ear and your belt cam, and if you go dark for more than sixty seconds, I pull the plug from the street and start a fire somewhere unpleasant."

Lucian perked up. *I like her fires.*

I pointed to the board. "We don't need a hero move. We need a key and a route."

Conner slid a keyring from a drawer. "We'll need luck, too."

"We make luck," I said.

Z's phone buzzed. She glanced, thumbed a reply, tucked it facedown. She caught me seeing it and lifted a shoulder. "She thinks I'm consulting at a conference. She also thinks I'm stubborn. Both true."

I nodded once. No lecture. No time.

We drilled the approach until the generator hiccupped, and the air went still for half a second. Conner banged the housing with a flat palm, and it settled. Z tuned the radio mic to a whisper so only the table heard it.

At dusk, we walked the perimeter again without crossing any lines. I timed the cart in my head as if I could drag it closer by force.

On the way back, a patrol truck rolled a block early. Conner saw it first, cut us into a doorway that smelled like bleach and old beer. We let it pass. Nobody breathed.

"Near-miss," Z muttered.

"Close enough," I said.

Back at the table, I ran the plan once more. No speeches. No edge. Just steps.

"Tomorrow we put on blue coveralls, push a cart, and borrow a door," I said. "In and out. If it goes sideways, we abort and try again. No pride."

Michael didn't argue. That told me more than any speech.

Z checked the time windows again and left the radio whispering. Conner locked the door and set his rifle by the frame.

I lay on the cot with my boots on, eyes open, counting minutes between inner-wing calls until the numbers blurred.

We weren't rescuing anyone yet. We were getting closer without getting killed. That had to be enough for one day.

Morning came gray, the kind of light that slipped through shutters like it already knew the day was going to get heavy. Conner was up first, same as always, checking his rifle, checking the locks, checking me. He didn't trust anything—not me, not Z, not the generator that kept coughing like it was one bad wire from dying.

Z looked like she hadn't slept at all. Hair pulled back, hoodie half-zipped, laptop humming beside her like it was breathing for her. The radio still whispered on the table, catching fragment, outer ring banter, forklift swears, somebody laughing too loud. All noise. Nothing useful yet.

I rolled off the cot, boots already laced. Michael stirred inside, the strategist, the one who hated waiting more than I did. I shoved him back. Not yet. His time was coming, but not yet.

Z glanced up from the screen, her eyes sharp but tired. "Cart run clocked again. Same sequence. Towels, water, stretcher. They're creatures of habit. Tonight's our hole."

Conner dropped a bundle of fabric onto the table. Blue coveralls. Faded, grease-stained, stinking of old soap and sweat. Real maintenance gear, not costume. "These get you through the first glance," he said flat. "After that, you're on your own."

I picked one up, held it against my chest. Fit close enough. Michael pushed harder inside, his voice steady. *You need me for this.*

Not yet, I told him. This was walking, not fighting. My work.

Z slid a small case across the table. Inside, a pinhole camera, a wire, and a comm bud. "Belt cam for Conner, ear for you. I'll see what you see, hear what you hear. You've got sixty seconds of silence before I pull fire. Don't make me pull fire."

Conner grunted like he didn't trust tech, but he clipped the cam anyway.

I pulled the radio closer, listening. Static bled into chatter. Then, clear enough to tighten my gut:

"—hallway two, guard exchange—"
"...water, towels..."

Same window. Same routine. Predictable enough to plan. Predictable enough to die if we got cocky.

Z leaned back, arms crossed. "Timing is clean. But if you hesitate, if you blink—"

"I don't blink," I said.

Lucian chuckled lazily in the back of my head. *That's Michael's line. Careful, Boy Scout. You're starting to sound like him.*

I ignored him.

Conner grabbed the map he'd drawn, tapped a square behind the admin wing. "Service corridor feeds into this dead space. Rats and dust, no cameras. You stash what you lift there until the wing rotates again. One hour, no more."

I nodded once. "Enough."

The room went quiet. Generator hum, radio whisper, jungle pressing in outside.

Z finally broke it, voice low. "Tonight's the night."

Michael leaned heavier inside, his presence colder, sharper. *Don't screw it up, Jace. If you do, I take the wheel whether you like it or not.*

I flexed my hands, steady. "We won't screw it up."

Not tonight.

False Faces

Jace

The coveralls stank of bleach and sweat, stiff at the seams like they hadn't been washed in a month. Conner tossed them on the table, and I pulled one over my clothes anyway. Blue was the language of men no one noticed.

Z taped the mic wire flat against my chest, fingers quick, impersonal. "Sixty seconds," she reminded me, voice low. "If you go dark, I burn something loud enough to drag the guards off you. Don't test me."

Conner grunted, sliding his arms through his own suit. "She means it."

The cart was dented metal on squeaky wheels, stocked with mop handles and buckets, bleach bottles rattling in the tray. Conner shoved it once to test the weight, then nodded. "It'll pass."

Z stood by the door, hood up, laptop clutched tight. "You're up. Don't bring me back a corpse."

We moved at shift change. Guards swapped posts, radios crackled with bored chatter, and the pier drowned itself in diesel noise. Blue coveralls blended into the hum. Conner pushed the cart. I walked alongside, posture loose, a bored janitor with somewhere else to be.

The first checkpoint didn't look at us twice. The badge we'd cloned yesterday lit green, beeped once. Gate opened. Inside the yard, the stink of fish and metal was stronger. Men in plainclothes barked orders at dockhands, but no one looked at us twice.

We skirted the admin wing. The service corridor loomed ahead, shadowed and narrow, ducts sweating condensation. Just like Conner said, No cameras, no lens.

We kept our pace steady. A guard leaned against the wall, smoking, glanced at us once, then back at the smoke curling from his lips. Nothing to see here.

Inside the corridor, the sound dropped. No engines, no chatter. Just the squeak of wheels and the steady drag of our boots.

"There," Conner murmured. He jerked his chin at a door marked *Mantenance*. A janitor stepped out, badge swinging from his belt, coffee in hand. He didn't see us until he almost walked into me.

"Pardon," I muttered, stepping aside, shoulder brushing his. My palm pressed the skimmer to his badge just long enough. The buzz in my hand told me it was done. Thirty seconds and I'd have Level 3.

The janitor grunted, walked off. Never looked back.

We kept walking until the corridor opened to a side hall. Conner slowed the cart, and I let us drift to a stop like we'd been meant to be there. I checked my watch. The timing matched what Z had written down — inner wing water run would pass this hall in five minutes.

We didn't need to see Madison. Not yet. Just confirm the pattern.

The radio on Conner's chest crackled. Voices rolled through — clipped orders, water, towels, stretcher. The same sequence. A cart rolled past the hall mouth, pushed by two uniforms. I didn't blink, just filed the timing away.

Conner shifted his grip. "We've got what we came for."

I nodded once. "Out."

We reversed the cart, rolling steady back through the corridor. Sweat slid down my spine under the coveralls, every step too loud, every squeak of the wheels like a scream. But no one stopped us.

The badge was ours. The route was confirmed. It was as clean as it was going to get.

Until it wasn't.

We hit the yard, floodlights buzzing, the noise of the pier swelling back around us. We were halfway to the outer gate when the crowd split. A man stepped into our path.

Not a grunt. Not a dockhand. His uniform was sharper, his boots newer, his eyes colder. Marco's second.

He looked at the cart. At the coveralls. At me. His stare lingered too long.

"Stop," he said, voice flat. "Stop."

Conner's hands tightened on the cart handle. Z's warning from earlier echoed in my skull — *Sixty seconds.*

Michael sharpened inside me, already bracing. I tensed, calculating routes. Lucian stirred, grinning in the dark.

The second took one slow step closer. "Papers. Now."

The second's eyes didn't blink. His hand rested casually on the pistol at his hip, but the weight in his stare told me casual wasn't real.

Conner shifted the cart forward half an inch, like he was buying us motion, but the man's voice cut sharper. "I said stop."

We froze.

Michael pressed at the back of my skull. *Don't fight here. Too many eyes.*
I knew that. I wasn't about to start a war in the yard.

The second stepped closer, his shadow spilling over the cart. "Papers," he repeated, slow. He wanted us nervous. He wanted to feel it roll off us.

My jaw clenched. I gave him the blank stare of a man who'd been ordered to mop floors, not answer questions.

But I could feel the edge tightening. One wrong twitch and he'd know.

Lucian's voice slid up lazy from the dark. *You're wound too tight, Boy Scout. He's already sniffing it on you.*

Not now, I hissed back.

Now's exactly when, Lucian chuckled. *You don't bluff soldiers with silence. You bluff them with charm. With bullshit so smooth they're nodding before they realize they've agreed. That's me, sweetheart. Let me talk.*

I tightened my grip on the cart handle, knuckles pale. "We're maintenance," I said flat in Spanish, my accent too clipped, too stiff. "Supervisor sent us."

The second's gaze sharpened. He heard it. He weighed it.

Lucian purred. *He doesn't buy it. One more second and you'll have rifles on you. Step back, Jace. Smooth tongues saves bullets.*

Michael stayed quiet, but I could feel him too, steady, waiting, ready if it all went to fire.

The second leaned close, close enough I caught the smoke on his breath. "Names," he demanded.

My chest locked. My mouth was dry.

Lucian grinned in the dark. *Relax, Boy Scout. This is where I shine.*

(*Lucian*)

The switch was easy. Jace held on too long, clenched like a fist, but he loosened just enough for me to slip past. I stretched into the skin, rolled my shoulders, let the tension bleed out of my face. You want to look like you belong? Then you act like you don't care if you do.

The second's eyes were sharp, measuring. He expected sweat, a stammer, maybe a twitch. Instead, I gave him a lazy grin.

"Names?" he asked again, harder this time.

"Why?" I said back in his own tongue, smooth as rum. "So you can write us up for carrying towels too slow? Didn't know Marco promoted hall monitors."

His jaw ticked, just enough for me to see I'd hit something. The trick wasn't to fight. It was to annoy. Knock him off balance.

I leaned on the cart like I had all the time in the world. "Supervisor sent us. Inner wing's bleeding again. You want to explain to Marco why the stains don't come up before dinner, be my guest. But me?" I tapped the badge clipped casually to my chest. "I'd rather not die because you wanted to play twenty questions."

Z kept her head down, perfect, Conner held the line steady, but I could feel Jace seething behind my eyes. *You're poking him.*

Exactly, I thought back. *Better he thinks I'm an asshole than a ghost.*

The second studied me too long, the way men do when they can't decide if you're stupid or dangerous. His hand hovered at his pistol. Mine stayed loose at my sides, shoulders easy.

Finally, he spat to the side, muttered something under his breath, and jerked his chin toward the gate. "Move."

I smiled wider, because it wasn't permission. It was victory. "Knew you'd see reason," I said, giving him a wink as I shoved the cart forward.

We rolled past, slow enough to feel his eyes burning holes in my back.

Only when the gate shut behind us did I let the grin drop. Inside, Jace snapped, *you nearly got us shot.*

"Please," I muttered under my breath. "I got us waved through. You'd still be explaining your accent."

And I kept pushing the cart, whistling low, like it had all been easy.

The cart rattled too loud on the cobblestones, but nobody stopped us. I kept the lazy grin plastered on my face until we were two streets clear, then let it slip into the smirk I actually meant.

Conner's eyes cut sideways, sharp as a knife. He didn't say a word, but I felt it. He was watching me — not just what I did, but how I carried it. Too loose. Too easy. Not Michael.

Jace snarled from the back of our skull, *He knows. He can tell.*

Let him, I thought back, keeping my shoulders loose, my stride easy. *Better he learns sooner than later.*

The safe house swallowed us again, shutters closed, generator humming. Z dropped her bag onto the table and powered up the laptop. Conner didn't sit. He stood in the middle of the room, arms folded, eyes locked on me like he'd just pinned a bug to a board.

"Not the same," he said flat. "Who the hell are you?"

I chuckled, leaning against the edge of the table. "You're sharper than I gave you credit for."

Z held up a hand quick, stepping between us. "Conner, don't—"

"No," he snapped. "I've been watching him since the strip. He changes. Posture. Voice. Even the way he breathes. That wasn't Michael out there." His eyes cut to me again, hard. "So, who am I talking to right now?"

I spread my hands, lazy, easy. "Lucian."

Z winced, rubbed at her temple. "This is going to sound insane—"

Conner barked a laugh, sharp and humorless. "Insane? My little sister just brought a man into my city who changes faces without changing skin. That's not insane, that's a problem."

I leaned forward, grin sharp. "Or it's an advantage."

Conner's jaw flexed. "Prove it."

Z exhaled hard, then looked at me. "Do it," she muttered.

Inside, Jace bristled. *Not like this.*

Michael's voice came steady, heavy. *Better he sees than keeps guessing.*

I smirked. "Fine. Show-and-tell."

And I stepped back.

Jace slid forward first, posture tightening, eyes narrowing, every movement clipped and controlled. "Jace," he said simply, voice low but firm.

Then Michael pressed through, spine straighter, gaze sharp as a blade. "Michael." His tone carried weight, the kind Conner would recognize in any soldier.

Finally, I let myself slip forward again, rolling my shoulders, grin easy, voice smooth. "Lucian. The one who just saved your ass on that strip."

Conner stared, jaw locked, eyes flicking between us like he was cataloguing every shift. Z finally spoke, voice softer. "They're all real, Conner. Separate, but one. Michael. Jace. Lucian. And…" She hesitated.

I caught it. The absence. The chair left empty.

Conner noticed too. "And what?"

Michael didn't answer. Neither did Jace.

I smirked, but it didn't reach my eyes. "The fourth's gone quiet."

Z met my gaze, steady. "Not gone. Just…we don't know."

Conner's eyes didn't leave me, even when Z shifted closer like she thought she could take the heat out of the room.

"So that's it," he said finally, voice low, sharp. "Three men in one body."

I let the smirk curl, leaning back like his rifle wasn't even there. "Not three men. One man, many edges. Michael the strategist, Jace the Boy Scout, and me, the one who keeps the tongue sharp when blades aren't enough. Parts of a whole, Hermano. Not masks. Not fakes. Just as real as you."

His jaw flexed like he was chewing glass. "And the fourth?" he pressed. "Don't tell me I imagined it. Z said four."

The air in the room turned thick, heavy. Silence stretched long enough for the generator hum to crawl into the gaps. I held his stare, lazy smile still painted on my face. "If he were here, you wouldn't be asking. You'd already know. He's quiet now. That's all you need."

Conner's eyes narrowed. "Quiet, or hiding?"

I leaned forward slowly, elbows on my knees, letting the smirk drop just enough to sharpen the edge in my voice. "If he were hiding, you wouldn't be sitting there breathing easy. Trust me on that."

Z blew out a breath, arms crossing tight, but I didn't give her the floor. This was mine.

Conner shook his head once, muttering, "This is madness."

"Madness," I echoed, grin slipping back like it never left, "is what's kept your sister alive long enough for you to complain about it."

"If you burn my city down," he said finally, voice flat as stone, "sister or not, I'll put a bullet in you before Marco does."

I chuckled low, leaning back again like the chair was a throne. "You'll have to get in line."

He didn't answer, just turned to check the bolt on the door and sat, rifle balanced across his knees, eyes still locked on me like he was waiting for the first slip.

I smirked, lazy but certain. I'd make sure he'd never get one.

Blue Cart, Black Blood

Lucian

Conner didn't sleep after that talk. I could tell by the way his boots never came off, rifle always within reach, eyes cutting at me like I'd sprout horns if he blinked. Z tried to fill the silence with the hum of her laptop, but even she felt it — her brother watching me like a live grenade left on the table.

I stretched out on the cot anyway, hands laced behind my head, grin painted on just to piss him off. "You'll wrinkle your face if you keep scowling at me like that, Hermano."

He didn't bite. Just poured coffee black and strong enough to melt metal, shoved a mug toward Z, and kept his rifle balanced across his lap.

"You trust him?" he asked her finally, never looking at me.

Z blew on the steam, took a sip, and didn't answer right away. That silence said more than words.

"Trust isn't the word," she said at last, setting the mug down. "But he's kept us alive this far. That counts for something."

I let the smirk widen. "Hear that? Kept you alive. You're welcome."

Conner's jaw tightened. He didn't thank me. Didn't even blink.

The radio cracked static before either of them could fire back. "…pasillo dos, cambio de guardia… enfermería solicita agua, toallas…" Same words, same routine. Proof that Madison was still breathing — or bleeding. Both, probably.

Z scribbled the time, slid the note across the table. "The cart run is clean. Tonight's our shot."

Conner grunted. "Then suit up."

He dropped the coveralls onto the table, blue and stinking of bleach and sweat. Real maintenance gear, not costume this time. I pulled one on slow, rolling my shoulders into it, letting the smell cling like smoke.

"You look like you've done this before," Z muttered, eyes flicking to me.

I winked. "Janitors. Gangsters. Politicians. Different uniforms, same bullshit."

Conner checked the wheels on the cart, gave it a shove. Metal squealed, buckets rattled. It sounded like work, which meant it sounded right. He glanced at me finally, his stare still sharp. "You screw this up, you don't get another chance."

I leaned on the cart, lazy grin hiding the coil in my gut. "Relax, Hermano. Smooth tongues open doors faster than bullets. Tonight, we prove it."

We rolled at dusk, blue coveralls, dented cart, the smell of bleach riding ahead of us like a hall pass. Z's voice sat in my ear, low and clean. "Inner net just called towels on pasillo dos. You've got eight minutes before the stretcher rolls."

Conner pushed the cart. I walked point, badge swinging lazy on my chest. Michael wanted tighter lines. Jace wanted cleaner timing. I wanted a bored face and a mouth that never apologized.

Gate one went green on the first swipe—Álvarez, Level 3. Z's clone sang sweet. We slid past a knot of plainclothes and a supervisor yelling about pallets like the apocalypse was made of wood.

The service corridor breathed cold. No cams—Conner had that right. Concrete sweat on the walls, lights buzzing like flies. We drifted with the cart, wheels squeaking a rhythm that said "maintenance" in any language.

"Left," Z breathed. "Archive duct is twenty meters. Dead space on the grid."

We hit MANTENIMIENTO. I palmed the latch, let the door swing enough to flash shelves: rags, acids, keys hooked like teeth. Good to know. Not tonight.

The archive room was dust and paper rot. Conner boosted me; I popped the vent, slid the mesh aside. He handed up the stash—two cover sheets, a roll of tape, the spare badge, a coil of thin line—and I tucked them into the duct's throat. Tomorrow's trick had a hidey-hole now.

Z again, quick. "Water call. Seven minutes."

Out. Cart rolling, faces bored. A guard with a cigarette gave us the nod that means "invisible." I nodded back with the look that means "you never saw me."

Inner hall next—clean floors, sick light. I counted doors because Jace is right: clocks and doors keep you breathing. Four to admin, three to infirmary, two more and you hit inner cells.

We didn't need to see her. We needed the route. Still, down the cross-corridor I caught the edge of a chair leg bruised brown. Old blood. Fresh scrub. I let my gaze slide off like I'd never learned the color.

"Stretcher in five," Z warned. "Don't get caught in the mouth."

We backed the cart to the service T and stood like men waiting on orders. The inner cart came—two uniforms, one bored medic, wheels with good bearings. Their chatter drifted past: "…again…blood on the chair…" Routine cruelty. Useful timing.

"Go," Z said. "You've got your mark."

We turned the cart and threaded for the yard. All easy until it wasn't.

And there he was. *God,* I thought, *not this oaf again.* Marco's second, stepping into our lane like he'd been waiting his whole life for the chance to look important. Same pressed boots, same cold stare he thought would make men fold. He didn't scare me yesterday, and he sure as hell wasn't about to scare me now.

The crowd parted around him like he owned the place. He carried himself like steel was jewelry, like his belt buckle meant something. All I saw was a man trying too hard to look like the wolf when he was just another dog on a leash.

Same man as yesterday. Different temperature.

He didn't raise his voice. Didn't have to. "You. Stop."

Conner's knuckles tightened white on the handle. Jace, in the back of my skull, went statue-still. Michael sharpened like a drawn edge.

I smiled like I had all night. "What's up, boss? You want the report now, or after we're done swimming in shit in corridor four?"

A flick at the corner of his mouth. Not amusement. Annoyance. Good.

"Papers," he said.

I patted my chest like I'd forgotten where I kept lungs, let the badge swing into his eye line, flipped it up with a knuckle so he had to step in to see. He did. Men like him always do.

While he read what he thought he wanted, I kept talking. Not fast. Smooth. "Maintenance. Álvarez sent us. He said if the smell reaches the dining hall, you sign the complaint. Doesn't matter to me, but you know how he loves paperwork."

Z whispered, barely air. "Name drop checks out on the net. Álvarez yelled two minutes ago. Good cover."

The second's gaze crawled from the badge to my face, trying to pin the shape of me to a file he didn't own. He didn't find it. He didn't like that.

"What fight?" he said.

I grinned wider. "The usual. Hall four. Security boys play boxing with people, we mop up the blood, everyone's happy. Except the drains." I jerked a thumb back at the cart. "I've got enough bleach to baptize half the island. You gonna let us work, or do you want to smell it yourself?"

He hated me. Perfect. Hate burns hotter than suspicion if you feed it right.

He looked past me at Conner. Conner looked like a wall that could shoot. The second looked at the cart, the buckets, the scuffed wheels that don't lie. He tasted the night, weighed his pride against the stink I'd promised.

A new voice clipped in on his radio: "Señor, stretcher coming through hall two. They need the way cleared."

Thank you, habit.

He clicked his tongue, stepped one pace left, and cut us a lane with his chin. "Rápido."

"Always," I said, and pushed the cart past hard enough he had to shift his foot or get hit. Petty? Maybe. Satisfying? Always.

We didn't breathe until the floodlight buzz softened and the yard was behind us. Even then, I kept the whistle low on my lips and the roll in my shoulders. Don't sprint when you're winning. Walk.

Two streets, then three. Fish rot and diesel gave way to wet leaves and generator hum. Conner didn't speak. Z's line stayed live in my ear, but she said nothing either. I could feel them both watching me—their silence like fingers on a pulse.

Safe house door, bolt, air that tasted like old coffee and gun oil. The cart's squeak died at the table. Z peeled her hood back and killed the feed. Conner set the rifle down slow, as if weight had nothing to do with gravity.

He didn't thank me. He didn't threaten me. He just looked, long enough to peel the grin off my face by force if it would come. It didn't.

Z broke the quiet first. "Route's clean. Duct's stashed. Level 3 held on both doors." She lifted her eyes to mine. "And you bought us thirty seconds we didn't have."

Conner said nothing for another beat. Then: "Tomorrow you don't buy seconds." He tapped the map, the inner hall we'd ghosted traced in greasy pencil. "Tomorrow you steal a person."

Michael pressed forward at that, the strategist banging knuckles on the table from the inside. He wanted angles. He wanted contingencies. He wanted to count bullets and bones.

I let him want. "We've got the seam," I said. "Towels, water, stretcher. We dress the cart right, we roll in, we roll out. Quiet."

Z snagged a marker, circled our duct stash. "I'll tune the mic for infirmary cadence, cut you a soft ping when stretcher passes admin. And I'll fork their badge DB, so your Level 3 reads as three different cleaners, not one."

Conner dragged a battered duffel up and unzipped blue coveralls, fresh cuffs, a canvas sling. "You'll need a reason to be near cells with a cart. Mop heads and a broken plunger."

I nodded. "Biohazard pickup. Bags, labeled. If they ask, we're pulling soiled linens, not saints."

Z didn't smile. "And if they don't ask?"

"Then we don't talk," I said. "We move."

The radio gave a last crackle like a dying insect, then fell quiet under Z's hand. The generator coughed, settled. Outside, the jungle said nothing at all.

I stretched the kinks out of my back, let the grin come back because that's the face I wear when the table wants to flinch. "Get some sleep," I said, and Conner's glare said he'd rather chew glass. "Tomorrow we make a mess no one can smell until we're gone."

Jace pressed up like a palm at my shoulder—wary, tight, ready to count doors again. Michael leaned in with his cold math. Somewhere deep, the empty chair stayed empty.

Good. Let the storm starve one more night.

Tomorrow, we'll feed it properly.

Z

The generator hummed low, steady for once, like even it knew none of us had patience for another sputter tonight. The map was a mess of pencil lines and grease smudges. My laptop hissed with code, the mic feed rolling in stuttered Spanish — towel, water, stretcher, rinse, repeat. Same damn cadence we'd been chasing for days.

Conner checked his rifle for the fourth time, jaw locked. Across from him, Lucian lounged in the same body, grin lazy, like this was theater and only he got the punchline.

Except I saw it — the grin shift, the eyes cut sharp like he was mid-argument with voices I couldn't hear. Then his mouth moved, quiet but clear.

"Ok."

And just like that, the grin fell away. Shoulders squared, pacing clipped. Not Lucian anymore. Jace.

"You don't hide as well as you think," I said, shutting my laptop half an inch.

He froze mid-step, jaw tight. "Didn't mean to."

"Doesn't matter," I said. "I can always tell."

His eyes flicked toward Conner — still cleaning his rifle like none of this existed — then back to me. "Lucian was pushing. Michael too."

I tilted my head. "And?"

Jace exhaled through his nose, controlled. "We talked. Came to an agreement."

Something in my stomach tightened. "What kind of agreement?"

"That I take point tomorrow. Infiltration's mine. Timing, movement, eyes." He tapped two fingers against his temple. "Michael stays back. Stays ready. If it turns, if things get loud… he takes the wheel."

I studied him, the clipped lines of his body, the way he said it like it wasn't up for debate. "So, Boy Scout leads, and Soldier waits in the wings."

"Exactly."

"And Lucian?"

He looked past me, toward the wall, a flicker of irritation ghosting across his face. "He'll talk his way into it if he can. He always does."

I leaned back in my chair, arms crossed, trying not to let the ache in my chest slip through my voice. "And HIM?"

Jace didn't answer right away. He just kept pacing, steps even, jaw set. Finally, quietly, "Still nothing."

The words sat between us heavier than the generator hum. I nodded once, slow, then pushed the laptop open again just to give my hands something to do. Numbers scrolled. Code whispered. None of it mattered.

I missed him.

Not the soldier. Not the Boy Scout. Not the smooth-tongued devil. *HIM.* The way he'd crack a joke sideways when no one else was listening. The way he made even silence feel alive, dangerous but… real. One of my best friends, even if I'd never admit that out loud to Conner. Now it was like a chair missing from the table, and we all pretended the legs still held steady.

I caught Jace's reflection in the laptop screen — shoulders pulled tight, pacing measured like he was counting tiles. He'd keep moving all night if I let him.

"You'll burn yourself out before tomorrow," I said.

His voice came back even but clipped. "Better me than the plan."

I didn't argue. Couldn't. Because the truth was, we needed both — the plan and him sharp enough to carry it.

Still, the ache in my chest didn't fade.

HIM was gone. And I hated that I couldn't tell if the silence meant safe... or locked away forever.

Jace finally stopped pacing, braced his palms on the edge of the table, and leaned over the map like the lines might shift if he glared hard enough. His voice was low, measured. "We only get one clean run. After that, Marco doubles every checkpoint."

Conner didn't look up from his rifle. "Then don't miss."

The room went quiet again, thick with tension. I closed the laptop all the way, shoved it aside, and dragged my chair closer to the map. "We won't. But I'm not walking you blind. Tomorrow isn't just your clock, Jace. It's mine too. I'll be in your ear the whole way."

His jaw tightened, but he gave a small nod. Agreement.

Conner finally set the rifle down, leaned back, arms crossed. His eyes cut between us, sharp enough to slice. "You two keep playing switcheroo, you're gonna slip in front of the wrong man. Then we're all dead."

Jace straightened, spine stiff. "That won't happen."

"Better not," Conner muttered, grabbing his mug. The coffee inside had gone cold, but he drank it anyway, like bitterness was the only thing keeping him upright.

I looked back at Jace, softer now. "You're steady. Just remember — it's not just you walking in there. It's all of us. Every damn edge of you."

For a second, his shoulders eased, and I thought maybe he'd say something human back. Instead, he just nodded once, clipped, and went back to studying the map.

Jace bent over the map, pencil in hand, marking routes cleaner than Michael's heavier cuts. Every line was measured, deliberate, like he'd already walked them twice in his head. Conner tracked the movement with a soldier's eye, but he didn't interrupt. Just cleaned his rifle slow, deliberate, the way men do when their hands want to hit something else.

"You're cutting the admin wing too close," I said, leaning in.

Jace shook his head. "It's cover, not a risk. Hall's blind for ninety seconds after water call. We use it."

"And if the cart drags?"

"Then we abandon. Duct stash, regroup." He didn't flinch when he said it, didn't soften it. To him, failure was math, not blood.

Conner set the rag down on the table, finally speaking. "You've got a lot of faith in seconds."

Jace's eyes flicked up, steady. "Clocks keep you alive. Lose count, you're dead."

Conner stared at him longer than he should've, jaw flexing, but he didn't argue. Not out loud.

I scribbled notes in the margin of my pad, fingers drumming against the table. "Fine. Ninety seconds through admin. Water call sets it. What's your trigger if it shifts?"

"The stretcher," Jace said without looking up. "If it rolls early, we know they've changed protocol. We abort. No heroics."

Conner grunted. "You sound like Michael."

"No," Jace said, calm but clipped. "Michael would try to fix it. I don't. I cut and run."

That silenced the room for a beat. The generator hummed, the radio hissed faint. I studied him — squared shoulders, clipped tone, lines sharper than Michael's cold weight or Lucian's loose grin. He believed what he was saying.

I closed my notebook. "Then tomorrow, you set the clock. We follow it."

Jace shifted the pencil across the map again, marking a dotted line through the service hall like he was carving it into stone. "Cart hits the inner wing here, pauses ten seconds for the water drop. Any longer, we stand out."

I leaned forward, tapping the square he'd circled. "What about the guard posted near the infirmary junction? He wasn't in the last rotation."

"He's a floater," Jace said. "Watched him twice. He'll move if you give him space."

"Or if he doesn't?"

"Then Conner's wall routine works. Block his sight, keep walking."

Conner snorted, not looking up from the rifle. "Not much of a plan if the whole thing depends on me looking broad."

"You are broad," I muttered, scribbling another note.

Conner shot me a look sharp enough to cut, but Jace spoke before it could flare. "It's not about size. It's about intent. Guards don't challenge men who move like they belong. You block the sightline, I handle the clock. Z feeds the net. It holds."

I exhaled, watching the way he said it. No hesitation. Michael would've layered contingency over contingency. Lucian would've made it sound like theater. Jace? He just laid it out like it was already written.

I shut my laptop fully now, folding my arms. "You realize tomorrow isn't a dry run anymore. It's not radios and badges and easy lies. It's a person. If it goes wrong, we don't get a second try."

Jace didn't blink. "I know."

Conner's jaw flexed, hands still working the bolt. "And if it does go wrong?"

Jace finally looked at him, steady. "Then I take the hit."

That stopped even Conner for a moment. He watched Jace like he was trying to decide if he believed him, then went back to his rifle without a word.

The silence stretched too long. The only sound was the radio hissing low, a voice muttering about pallets, then static again.

I drummed my fingers against the table, finally saying what none of them wanted to. "We only get one shot at this. If we miss... Madison doesn't get another night."

The silence pressed too heavy, like the generator hum was the only heartbeat in the room. Jace leaned back over the map, drawing another line like it mattered more than air.

Conner just kept running the bolt, over and over, metal on metal.

I slammed my palm flat on the table. "Do you two even hear yourselves?"

Both their heads snapped up, but I didn't give them a chance to speak. The words tumbled too fast, sharp, heavy.

"You're talking like this is a goddamn drill. Like it's mops and radios and who walks wider down a hallway. Do you get it? Do you really get it? This isn't a test anymore. Madison's in there bleeding every single day while you sit here drawing arrows on paper like it'll magically make her whole again."

Jace's jaw tightened, but I kept going.

"What if the badge doesn't scan? What if the cart squeaks too loud? What if the guard you call a 'floater' decides he's in the mood to play hero tomorrow? What if they check the duct, what if they pull the mic, what if the stretcher doesn't come when it's supposed to? What if she's not even in the same hallway by the time we get there? What if you're wrong, Jace? What if Michael's wrong? What if Lucian can't talk his way out of it?"

Conner set the rifle down hard, but I steamrolled right over the sound.

"You all act like you've got time to make mistakes. You don't. We don't. One slip and it's over. For her. For all of us. Do you even understand that? Or are you all so wrapped up in playing soldier and spouting plans that you've forgotten what's actually on the line?"

The room went still after that, my breath coming too fast, my hands shaking against the edge of the table.

Jace didn't snap back. Didn't bristle. He just stood there, shoulders squared, eyes locked on mine with that clipped steadiness. "I do understand. That's why I'm the one going in."

I barked a laugh, sharp and ugly. "Bullshit. If you understood, you wouldn't be so calm about it."

That hit. His eyes flashed, reminding me of HIM, sharp as glass, and for once the metronome cracked. "Calm? You think this is calm?" He jabbed a finger at the map, the pencil lines carved over and over like scars. "Why the hell do you think I've been standing here staring at this for the hundredth time? Why do you think I've run every route in my head until I can't close my eyes without seeing them?"

I flinched, but he didn't stop.

"You think I don't hear her in there too? Every time the radio spits out 'towels, water, stretcher' I picture it. I picture her strapped down and bleeding, and I add it to the clock in my head. Tick. Tick. Tick. You want to know why I'm quiet, Z? Because if I let myself say it out loud, it won't stop. It'll eat me alive before we even get to the gate."

The words hit hard, louder than the generator, louder than the jungle pressing at the walls. He shoved the pencil down on the table so hard it snapped, the lead rolling across the map like a dead thing.

Conner's hand hovered near his rifle, but he didn't move, didn't say a word.

I opened my mouth, but nothing came out.

Jace leaned over the map, breath steadying slowly, like he was forcing the storm back under his skin. "So don't tell me I'm not taking it serious. This is all I take serious. Every second of it."

The broken pencil rolled to the edge of the map. None of us touched it.

I leaned back in my chair, arms tight across my chest, pulse still spiking. "Fine," I said finally, not soft but not swinging anymore. "Then prove it tomorrow. Make all those clocks in your head mean something."

Jace's jaw flexed, but he didn't answer. Just bent over the lines again, shoulders squared like the weight belonged there.

The room held its silence — not empty, not calm, just heavy enough that even the generator's hum felt like it was listening.

Ash and Iron

Madison

The room pressed in heavy, like it wanted me smaller. Like if I shrank enough, I'd disappear into the stains under my boots. The straps at my wrists burned raw, but even that was dull now — just another ache in a body that had too many.

I tilted my head back against the chair, let the ceiling blur until it was just a wash of gray. No stars. No sky. Just cement and the faint drip of water somewhere behind the wall. Time wasn't real here. It stretched, twisted. I could've been here days or years and it would feel the same.

My throat was dry enough to crack, tongue thick like ash. They wanted me thirsty. Wanted me begging. But all it did was sharpen me. Made every thought scrape harder, made every memory come with edges.

Michael's face. The storm in his eyes. The way his voice had changed when he wasn't just Michael anymore. Jace's steadiness. Lucian's grin. HIM. God help me, even HIM.

I closed my eyes, let the ghosts flicker across the inside of my skull. Sometimes I swore I could hear them. Not here, not in this room — but close, like they were just one wall away.

Marco thought I was alone. That's what kept him smiling. That's what made him walk in here like he owned me.

But he didn't know. He didn't understand that even strapped to this chair, I wasn't by myself. I carried them with me. Every voice, every shadow. Even the one I'd sworn terrified me most.

My lips cracked when I whispered it, too soft for the guards outside to hear.

"You're not gone. Not any of you."

And I made myself believe it.

The words hung in the stale air, too thin to matter, too sharp to take back. My throat tore on them, but the silence after was mine. It was the only thing Marco hadn't stolen yet.

Boots scuffed outside the door. Not the bored shuffle of guards killing hours. Heavier. Slower. Purpose in the weight of each step.

The lock ground metal against metal. A pause, like whoever stood there wanted me to hear the teeth catch. To know what was coming before it came.

I kept my head tilted back, eyes on the ceiling. I wouldn't give him the satisfaction of seeing me strain at the straps.

The hinges screamed when the door opened. Cold air slipped in with him, carrying cologne sharp enough to cut through blood and mildew.

Marco filled the doorway like he had all the time in the world. He didn't hurry. He never hurried. His monsters never needed to.

I swallowed against the rawness in my throat, forced my lips to curl bloody and cracked into something like a smile.

"Here to check if I've broken yet?"

His shadow stretched across me, long and patient, as he stepped closer.

Marco didn't answer me right away. He just crouched low, the way he liked, so his face was level with mine. His suit was too clean for this place, cuffs sharp, silver watch catching the single bulb's sick light. He smelled like money and blood.

His hand settled on the arm of the chair, casual. Too close. Too heavy.

"Tell me, Madison," he said, voice smooth, almost gentle. "Where is it?"

My lips stuck when I tried to smile again. My mouth was too dry, too cracked, but I forced it anyway. "Same place it's always been. Out of your reach."

His eyes flickered, narrowing just enough to break the mask. He leaned in, thumb brushing a streak of blood from my cheek like he owned it.

"Cute. But I'm not asking where it isn't. I'm asking where it is. Because you know. And sooner or later, you'll tell me."

I shook my head, slowly, because it was all I could manage. "You'll die trying first."

The smile came back to his face, patient, practiced. He straightened, adjusting his cuffs like I hadn't spoken at all.

"I don't need you to tell me," he said. "You will, eventually. But maybe not today. Because today…" His eyes sharpened, cruel. "…I'd rather tell you about your friends."

My chest pulled tight. I didn't let it show, but he saw anyway. He always did.

He stepped behind me, voice brushing my ear. "The soldier. The boy scout. The smooth tongue. Even the monster. They're close to breaking."

I froze. My heart hammered so loud it drowned the hum of the light.

"No," I rasped.

"Yes," he breathed. "Do you know what a man looks like when he thinks he's stronger than chains? When he realizes steel always wins? They look just like him. Just like your precious Michael. Just like the others. Sweat. Blood. Eyes wide. And then… silence."

I shook my head again, harder this time, the straps burning my wrists raw. "You're lying."

He chuckled low. "Am I?" He moved back into view, crouched in front of me again, close enough I could see the faint scar at his throat where one of them had once tried to end him. His eyes glittered, feeding on every crack in my breath.

"They're close, Madison. One more night. One more turn of the screw. Then they'll beg me. And when they do, you'll hear it. You'll know you weren't worth the fight."

I bit down hard, tasted blood, forced the smile back onto my lips even though it hurt. "You can break chains. You can spill blood. But you'll never break them."

His hand shot out, gripping my jaw, squeezing until my teeth ached. "We'll see."

His grip stayed, thumb digging into the swell of my cheek until spots flared in my good eye.

"You think I can't?" Marco's voice dropped lower, colder. "You've seen me do worse for less."

I tried to shake my head, but his hand pinned me still. My throat worked around words that barely scraped out.

"They don't... break like that."

He smirked, cruel, like I'd just handed him a secret. "That's the part you don't understand. Everyone breaks. Some just take longer."

He released me with a sharp shove. My head snapped back against the chair, stars bursting white. When my vision cleared, he was pacing slowly in front of me, hands behind his back, calm again — too calm.

"You still think they're close," he said. "That they're coming for you. But I've seen the truth. Their eyes are already faltering. The boy scout sweats. The soldier clenches his teeth. The smooth one can't talk his way out of iron."

He turned, crouched back down, face level with mine, eyes bright with mock pity. "Even the monster you fear... he's quiet now. Do you feel it? Empty. Hollow. He's not coming."

The words sliced deeper than any fist. My throat burned, a sound clawing its way up, but I forced it down. "You don't know them."

His smile widened. "I know enough. I know how men die. And when they do, you'll be the last thing on their tongues. A curse. Not a prayer."

Something in me cracked. I felt it, hot in my chest, cold in my gut. I dropped my gaze to hide it, but he caught it — he always caught it.

"There it is," he whispered, savoring. "The flinch. The doubt." He stood, adjusted his cuffs like none of this mattered. "That's all I need. Doubt will do the work for me."

He nodded at the door. The guards shifted, boots heavy on the concrete, waiting for his word. He lingered one last moment, looking down at me like I was already his.

"Think of them tonight," he said. "Think of them begging. And when you're ready to trade the brooch for their screams to stop... call for me."

My lip split wider as I smiled, blood in my teeth. "Oh, I'll think of them," I rasped. "But not the way you want."

Marco froze mid-step, just enough for me to see the twitch in his jaw.

"Yeah," I pushed, voice raw but steady. "I'll think about Jace's hands on me, Michael's mouth on my neck, Lucian whispering sin until I couldn't breathe. I'll think about how every single one of them gave me more pleasure in a single night than you managed in your whole goddamn life."

His nostrils flared. He turned back slowly, mask cracking.

"You hear me?" My laugh came sharp, cracked, but I forced it out. "I came so many times I lost count. That's what I'll remember tonight. Not their screams. Their mouths. Their hands. Their heat."

He was in front of me again before I could blink, hand snapping to my throat, squeezing just enough to choke the sound. His eyes burned hot, mask gone, raw rage spilling through.

"Shut your mouth," he hissed.

I smiled wider, even with his grip cutting my breath. "Make me."

His teeth bared, hand trembling with the need to break something — me. For a moment I thought he might. For a moment I prayed he would. Because the longer I held his rage, the less he was looking at them. The more he was chained here with me.

The guards shifted uneasily by the door. Marco finally released me with a shove so hard the chair legs screeched across the concrete.

"You'll bleed for that," he spat, straightening his cuffs with shaking fingers.

I dragged a laugh out of my raw throat. "Already am."

He stormed out, door slamming, lock grinding home.

I sagged back, chest heaving, throat bruised under his hand. My wrists burned, my mouth tasted of blood and iron, but I'd done it. I'd kept him here. Kept him focused on me.

I forced a whisper past the ache. "Worth it."

The word scraped out of me like gravel. I meant it, even as the chair dug into my spine and the air cut thin through my raw throat.

The door's slam still echoed in my skull long after he was gone. The silence that followed was heavier than his presence had been. It pressed down until my chest ached, until every pulse of my heartbeat felt like it was trying to tear its way out.

My wrists screamed with every twitch. I tested the straps once, twice, but the leather only bit deeper. Skin peeled raw. Wet. Sticky.

I let my head fall forward, hair matted to my cheek with sweat and blood. My breaths came jagged, like every rib wanted to splinter. The adrenaline that had carried me through his rage ebbed fast, and when it went, it took my strength with it.

The room swayed. The gray ceiling blurred. My vision stuttered dark around the edges. I clenched my jaw until my teeth ground together, trying to hold on. Trying not to give him the satisfaction of collapse, even when he wasn't here to see it.

My throat burned when I swallowed, bruises blooming under his grip, hot and swelling. My tongue tasted like rust.

I told myself not to cry. Not now. Not ever in front of him. But alone? Alone the tears came anyway, hot and silent, cutting clean tracks down skin smeared with blood.

"Worth it," I croaked again, weaker this time, as if saying it twice might make it truer.

My head lolled against my shoulder. Muscles too heavy to hold. The drip behind the wall ticked steady, cruel in its rhythm, reminding me time hadn't stopped just because I had.

I let the dark roll in, not sleep, not mercy—just the body's way of folding when it couldn't take another second upright.

Then—shouts. Muffled, sharp. Boots hammering against the corridor outside. One guard barking orders, another voice breaking high with panic. Radios squawking over each other, the edge of fear cutting through the static.

Something had shifted. Something big.

My vision tunneled, black crowding out the gray. I wanted to hold on, to hear one more word, one more crack in their voices. But my body folded first.

Right before the dark rushed in, I heard the same words shouted, over and over again.

"¡La Sombra! ¡La Sombra!"

Infiltration

Jace

The safe house reeked of stale coffee and gun oil. Conner hadn't closed his eyes, Z hadn't looked away from her screen, and I'd worn grooves into the map with my fingertip until the lines lived behind my eyelids.

Heat pressed through the shutters as dawn bled gray into the room. The generator droned steadily in the corner, the one sound keeping us from hearing how tense we all were.

Z sat hunched over her laptop, shoulders stiff, chewing through code like she could force the net to cough up more. Conner was on his rifle again, checking and rechecking parts that didn't need it. He needed something to do with his hands.

Me? I stayed over the table, boots planted, finger tapping the duct we'd stashed gear in. The path was carved into me now: service corridor, archive vent, admin wing, infirmary pass. Eight minutes from towels to stretcher. That was the window. That was the seam.

Michael pushed forward in my head, steady but heavy. *You ready?*

My jaw locked. I didn't look up. *I'm ready.*

The words slipped out anyway. Quiet. "I'm ready."

Z's eyes flicked up, sharp. She thought I meant her. "Good. Because tonight we stop watching and start pulling."

Conner grunted. "About time."

I stayed on the map, tracing the route one more time. My voice came out flat, controlled. "We go in quiet. We come out quiet. Anything else, it's done."

We didn't waste daylight.

Conner dragged the battered cart out from the corner, wheels squealing like it wanted to give us away before we left the door. Z handed me the coveralls, blue stiff with bleach and sweat. They stank like real work, which was the point.

I pulled mine on, zipped it to the collar, clipped the badge where it would swing easily. Conner checked the buckets and bottles in the tray, gave it one shove, and nodded. It sounded right — heavy, loud, and invisible all at once.

Z moved in close, fixing the wire flat against my chest. "Sixty seconds," she whispered. "If you go dark, I light a fire they can't ignore."

Conner's grunt was enough agreement. He slung his rifle inside the cart's frame, wrapped in rags. One quick motion and it would be in his hands.

The radio crackled once, then fell quiet. Timing lined up with the notes we'd been writing for days. Towels, water, stretcher. The cadence was already ticking in my head.

I pulled the door open. Morning hit damp and hot, the air thick with salt and diesel. Barceloneta was alive again, shutters slamming, vendors shouting, dogs nosing through trash. Marco's men were everywhere, posture stiff, eyes cutting too sharp for locals.

We rolled in steady. Blue coveralls. Dent in the cart. A badge swinging where people could see it. Invisible by being obvious.

First gate read green. A beep, a buzz, and we were through. Conner pushed; I walked point. Z's voice sat in my ear, low and clean. "Outer net's quiet. No chatter about you yet. Keep moving."

The service corridor opened like a throat, damp concrete, buzzing lights, no cameras. Our wheels squeaked in rhythm with our steps.

Conner kept his grip locked, shoulders square like he could push the weight of the whole city if he had to.

We cut past the first checkpoint. Guard didn't even look up, coveralls, badge, buckets. Just another shadow in the noise. That was the point.

Inside the service corridor, the air changed. Quieter. Cooler. Concrete walls sweating damp, lights buzzing overhead like flies. Every squeak of the wheels landed too loud. Every bootstep echoed back.

"Left, twenty meters," Z's voice slid in my ear, clipped. "Archive duct. Still a dead zone."

I glanced once, quick. The door marked MANTENANCE hung crooked, paint peeling. Good place to disappear if we needed it. Not tonight.

We kept rolling until the archive room yawned open. Dust, mold, shelves sagging under forgotten files. Conner boosted me; I popped the vent, stashed the bundle: spare badge, tape, covers, the coil of line. If we got chased, we'd have something hidden that might buy another run.

"Back on clock," Z warned. "Towels just hit net. Seven minutes."

We pushed deeper. The corridor narrowed, turned slick with mop water someone hadn't bothered to drain. My boots whispered through it. Conner's cart wheels left twin lines glistening behind us. Tracks.

I kept my shoulders loose, face blank. Janitor bored with his life. Nothing more.

The admin wing ghosted past on our right — clean walls, doors locked tight. Beyond that, the hallway opened brighter, too clean, too controlled. The kind of space where mistakes got you noticed.

"Five minutes," Z whispered.

I didn't answer. Just tapped the cart once with my knuckle. Conner pushed. We were closing on the route.

The light changed again. Too bright, like someone had scrubbed the bulbs until they hurt to look at. The cart's squeak dragged louder in the open hall, no shadows to swallow us now.

Z's voice snapped in my ear. "Three minutes. Cam—"

Static bled over the rest, sharp and ugly. A hiss, then half a word, then nothing.

"Say again," I murmured, low. Nothing came back but the pop of interference.

Conner flicked his eyes at me, the smallest twitch, like he'd caught it too. His hands never left the cart.

I slowed my breathing, counted steps. Four doors, five. Timing was a rhythm I'd learned by heart, but without her feed, I couldn't hear the net. Couldn't confirm.

Static spit again in my ear. "sle… aisle—" Cut. Dead.

"Z," I whispered, jaw tight. "You're breaking up. I need the clock."

Silence.

Michael pressed sharp inside me, steady but heavy. Trust the rhythm. You counted it a hundred times.

I swallowed hard. The hall stretched in front of us, too clean, too bright, too loud.

Conner muttered without moving his mouth, eyes locked forward. "Do we keep?"

The carts wheels squealed again. My pulse kept time with them.

I clenched my jaw. "We keep."

The squeak of the cart bled into boots. Not ours. Different rhythm. Heavy. Close.

Conner's grip tightened on the handle. I lifted my chin just enough to catch the shadows cutting across the far end of the hall. Three men. No—four. Rifles slung, posture too sharp to be maintenance.

"Eyes down," I muttered, low. We couldn't double back. Corridor boxed us in. The cart was cover, but only once.

They spotted us quick. One barked in Spanish, clipped. "Stop! Credentials!"

Conner kept pushing, pace steady, like he didn't hear. It worked for three steps. Then the lead guard's voice snapped sharper. "I said stop!" Rifles lifted.

Conner froze. My pulse thudded steadily, but inside my chest Michael pressed hard against the wall. *Not yet,* I told him. *Too loud. Too many.*

I slid around the cart slow, badge swinging, bored mask fixed. "Maintenance," I said flat, voice even. "Supervisor's breathing down our necks. Blood in aisle four. You want the stink in your lunchroom?"

One guard sneered. The others didn't buy it. They fanned out, cutting the corridor into bars. The cart wasn't cover anymore. It was a trap.

Then the closest one shoved me. Hard. My shoulder hit concrete, badge clattering against my chest. His rifle jammed across my collarbone.

Reflex snapped before thought, I caught the barrel and twisted. He slammed me into the wall. Pain burst white down my arm. Another guard moved in. Conner dropped the cart with a crash, rifle half out of the rags before two more piled on him.

"Don't move!" one roared, boot slamming into Conner's ribs.

The world turned narrow. Fists. Rifles. Boots on concrete. I blocked, countered, moved sharp, but weight stacked fast. One got me in a choke, arm locked under my jaw. Pressure crushing my throat. Vision sparking.

The choke locked in deep, like iron against my windpipe. My nails clawed at the forearm across my throat, but the bastard had leverage, weight stacked clean. My boots scraped useless against the floor.

Ten seconds. Maybe less.

Pressure built behind my eyes. My chest heaved, but nothing came in. The world was shrinking to sparks.

Nine.

Conner's voice was somewhere behind the blur, muffled by fists and boots. Couldn't reach him. Couldn't even shout.

Eight.

The guard twisted harder. Pain streaked down my spine. My lungs screamed.

Seven.

Michael's presence pressed in my skull, steady, waiting. *Let me.*

Six.

I shook my head inside, desperate. *No. I can do it—*

Five.

Darkness licked the edges of my vision. My knees buckled.

Four.

You can't break it, Michael said. Calm. Certain.

Three.

Stars burst white. My body convulsed. My throat was on fire.

Two.

I gave up the fight to stay silent. In my head, in my gut, in whatever voice I had left, I roared it.

MICHAEL!

One.

The world cut clean. Like a switchblade slicing through the dark. The panic, the sparks, the blind clawing, gone. Everything sharpened. Every grip, every breath, every mistake in the bastard's stance lit up like a target.

Michael had the wheel. And the man choking me had no idea he was already dead.

(Michael)

The choke didn't vanish. Pressure still dug into my throat, his forearm a bar of iron. But now it was mine to read, mine to break.

His grip was too high. Thumb pressing wrong, heel planted lazy. I dropped my weight fast, sharp, teeth clenched. My elbow slammed back—ribs cracked under the blow. His grunt loosened the choke a breath too much. That was all I needed.

I wrenched sideways, caught his wrist, twisted until bone groaned. He screamed, but it cut short when I slammed him into the wall, shoulder-first. The pop of dislocation echoed down the corridor. He folded.

Another came in wild, rifle swinging like a bat. I stepped in, not back. Barrel caught, twisted. My boot hooked his ankle, drove him down hard. His jaw met concrete with a crack that sprayed blood across the floor.

Two more were still on Conner. One had his rifle pinned, the other raining boots into his ribs. They didn't see me move. They didn't hear me coming over their own noise.

First one caught my fist. Knuckles met cheekbone, bone gave first. He dropped like dead weight. The second turned, shock wide in his eyes. Too late. I drove the stolen rifle butt into his teeth, once, twice, until blood sprayed in a thick line down his chest.

Silence hit, heavy, broken only by the ragged breath of the ones still conscious enough to whimper. My own lungs dragged in clean air, throat raw but free.

Conner hauled himself up, ribs tight, blood running from his lip. His eyes found me. Locked on me. And I saw it in his face—he knew. This wasn't Jace anymore.

I straightened, rifle balanced easy in my hands, stance squared, breath steady. Cold filled me. Purpose. Precision.

Inside, Jace staggered, voice faint. *I had it—*

You were choking, I answered, iron-flat. *You were seconds from a blackout. Now it's my time.*

His silence told me he hated it. But he didn't fight me for the wheel.

The last guard still breathing tried to crawl backward, blood bubbling through broken teeth. I stepped over him, steady, eyes on the corridor ahead.

"Up," I said, voice clipped, cold. Not to him. To Conner.

Conner rose, rifle back in his grip. His stare burned into me, sharp, measuring. "That wasn't you before."

I didn't flinch. "It is now."

We moved forward, boots in step, leaving blood in the hall behind us.

(Z)

The feed cracked, spat, then died flat.

"Jace?" I snapped, fingers slamming keys. Nothing. The waveform stuttered, then blanked out.

I rerouted, killed the filter, boosted the gain. Static roared back so hard it made my ear buzz. No voices. No cadence. Just white noise.

"Fuck."

The map on my screen glowed cold blue, their trackers lagging, blinking one beat behind reality. I knew those halls. Knew the timing. Eight minutes from towels to stretcher, seven from stretcher to cells. But without their voices, I was blind.

I chewed the inside of my cheek, hard enough to taste copper. Two options: sit here and trust Jace's clock, Conner's gun, Michael's ghost — or get off my ass and make sure they had cover.

The choice should've been simple. Trust the plan. Stick to the plan.

Then the sound hit.

Sharp, jagged, distant but real. A crash like metal striking stone. Shouts spiking over each other in Spanish. Boots hammering faster than patrol rhythm.

My throat locked. That wasn't background noise. That was them.

"Shit, shit."

I was already yanking my hoodie up, slamming my laptop closed. My heart beat so hard it shook my hands, but I shoved the pistol into my waistband, grabbed the bag, and bolted.

Conner would've told me to wait. Jace would've told me to trust the math. Michael would've said it wasn't my fight.

But none of them were me.

I wasn't built to wait. I was built to bleed noise.

By the time I hit the street, my sneakers were slapping concrete, my lungs burning. The pier loomed ahead, floodlights buzzing, voices carrying sharp in the damp night air. I didn't think about subtle. I didn't think about diversions.

I thought about them.

So, I charged straight for the gate, ready to set the whole fucking board on fire if it bought them thirty seconds more.

The pier swallowed me in light and noise. Floodlamps buzzed hot against the night, guards shouting over crates and clattering chains. I pushed harder, lungs tearing, legs a blur.

"¡Stop!" a voice cracked sharp. Rifles turned. Boots thundered, not patrol, not rhythm — the chase.

No time to play small.

I veered into the open, hoodie up, bag clutched tight. "Cartel shit! Fire! Fire!" I screamed, voice ragged, wild Spanish enough to spike nerves.

It worked — for a breath. Men spun, rifles up, confusion slashing through order. Shouts tangled. A dozen eyes burned into me, none of them on the hall Jace and Conner had slipped through.

Then the crowd broke, and Marco walked through it.

Not running. Not shouting. Just walking, cufflinks shining under floodlight, eyes locked on me like I'd been dragged here just for him. His men didn't bark another word, they didn't have to. He raised a hand once, and they crushed me down.

Boots slammed into my ribs, rifles dug into my spine. My pistol skittered away, metal clattering. A baton cracked my forearm, hot white pain. They forced me up to my knees, arms wrenched back, face tilted into the glare.

And there he was, close enough for me to smell the cologne under the gun oil. Marco. Smiling like he'd just won twice.

"Always the loud one," he said, voice smooth as silk strangling. "Always desperate to matter."

I spat blood at his shoes. "Better to be loud than soft like you, bitch."

The crack came fast, his hand across my jaw. My head snapped sideways, copper in my mouth. The guards tightened their grip, waiting for the order.

Through the bodies, I saw them. Jace. Conner. Half-shadowed in the corridor that cut toward admin, eyes wide, locked on me. Hidden — but only if I kept them hidden.

I dragged air in, forced the words past my broken mouth. I shaped them slow, clear.

Stay.

I *love you.*

Jace shook his head, once, sharp. Conner looked like stone cracking.

Marco followed my gaze, then chuckled low, leaning close enough for his breath to warm my cheek. "Ah. So, you're still protecting ghosts."

He drew his pistol, casual, like swatting a fly. Pressed the muzzle under my chin, cold metal lifting my head until I stared into his eyes. "Then die for them."

The world slowed. I could hear the floodlamps buzzing, the guards shifting, my own pulse hammering. I could see Jace and Conner frozen, burning my face into theirs because this was the last time.

I smiled, blood wetting my teeth. "Fuck you, Marco."

He pulled the trigger.

Light and sound exploded, bone snapping white-hot. My body folded, knees hitting concrete, vision tilting sideways. Voices blurred, boots shifting back.

The last thing I clung to was their faces — Jace, Conner — still free, still unseen. My family.

And then nothing.

Return

HIM

The gunshot split me open.

For a breath I didn't move. Couldn't. The floodlamps burned, the guards shouted, Conner's boots scraped concrete, Jace's heart stuttered inside our chest — but none of it mattered. Because Z…..was gone.

The cage around me rattled like thunder. The Presence pressed down harder, iron and cold, the weight that had smothered me for so long. It wanted me silent. Wanted me buried.

But grief isn't quiet. Rage doesn't stay buried.

Shock rolled through me like fire, and I laughed once — a sound raw and broken, like I didn't even recognize it myself.

"Who am I supposed to talk to now?" My voice cracked against the bars, low and shaking. "When the others shut me out? When the night is too long and the voices won't stop?"

The wall pressed harder. I pushed back harder.

"Who's gonna remind me I'm still needed?" My hands curled, nails splitting against stone. "Who's gonna drag me out for ice cream and tell me to quit being an asshole? Who's gonna…"

I faltered. The cage shook. The Presence strained.

There was no answer. Just silence. Just her blood on the concrete.

I roared. The cage shaking with every strike of my fist.

"You can't," the Presence spoke. "You must remain here, let them do this. Jace, Michael, Lucian, they can do this."

But I wasn't listening. My fist hit harder, voice louder. I felt the cage give way. The iron split. The wall broke.

The Presence cracked, and I poured through. Not fast. Not all at once. Slow. Measured. Like smoke seeping through a locked door.

The guards froze. Rifles lifted, but not steady. Their eyes weren't on the gun in my hand or the blood at my boots. Their eyes were on *me*.

I tilted my head, slow, deliberate. Let them see the smile that didn't belong on a man. Too wide. Too patient.

One of them swallowed, voice trembling like it barely belonged to him. "La... La Sombra..."

The word spread like a sickness. Whispered, hissed, spat between teeth. *La Sombra.* The shadow they tell their kids about to keep them inside at night. The thing that lives in the cracks of Barceloneta.

I stepped forward once, and the floodlamps hummed louder, like even the wires knew something had slipped loose.

They didn't run. Not yet. Fear locks the legs before it frees them. And I wanted them locked. Wanted them staring.

"Say it louder," I whispered, my voice low enough it scraped their bones. "Say my name."

Another guard choked it out, louder this time. "¡La Sombra!"

The word hung in the air, torn between their teeth and the floodlamps. I let it sit. Just long enough for their pulses to trip over themselves. Then I moved.

The first one didn't even scream. My hand was in his collar, lifting, twisting — his throat gave under my grip like wet wood snapping. I dropped him before the others even raised their rifles.

The second fired wild, muzzle flash white in the dark. The round burned past my ear, close enough to sting. I was already on him. My palm crushed the barrel sideways, my other hand splitting his jaw open with a single strike. His rifle clattered useless, teeth pink on the floor.

The third tried to run. Smartest of them, but not smart enough. I caught the back of his vest, yanked him down hard, my boot grinding into his spine until it cracked. His scream carried down the corridor, sharp and panicked.

That was the moment it broke. The rest lost nerve. One dropped his rifle, another tripped over his own boots trying to flee. They weren't guards anymore. Just animals scrambling from fire.

And I laughed. Low, ragged, sharp in my chest. Z's blood was still hot in the air, and every drop of it screamed for this.

I grabbed another by the hair, dragged his face across the concrete until it painted red behind him. His voice cut off in a wet gargle. I left him twitching and stepped into the next.

They shouted orders I didn't care to hear, names I didn't care to learn. Bullets sparked off steel, ricocheted wild. Too slow. Too frantic. Their hands shook. My hands didn't.

One tried to beg. I saw his lips forming *por favor*. I split his skull against the wall before he finished.

The ground was slick now. Boots sliding in blood, air heavy with copper and cordite. I breathed it in, let it coat my tongue. Every scream, every shot, every break of bone was a hymn.

A rifle cracked from the far end. Not warning, not blind. A shot aimed clean.

I turned with it, felt the round tear past my ribs — hot, sharp, shallow. Didn't matter. Pain was just noise.

I was already moving.

The shooter's eyes widened as I closed the hall like it was nothing. He fired again, again, the muzzle flash burning desperate. One round grazed my shoulder, another sparked off the wall. Then I was on him.

I wrenched the rifle sideways, steel groaning under my grip, and slammed the stock into his chest. Once. Twice. Bone caved with the third. He folded around it like paper, wheezing red. I dropped the weapon and tore him open bare-handed.

The others were watching now. Backing away, whispering prayers they'd never said before.

I stepped through the blood, slow. Deliberate. Let them see me. Let them choke on it.

One bolted left, sprinting for the floodlit yard. I let him take three steps. Then my knife, when had I even drawn it, spun from my grip, burying itself in the base of his neck. He went down twitching, fingers clawing at nothing.

Another stumbled back into a stack of crates, kicking them over as he scrambled. His boots slipped in the gore, hands scrambling for a pistol. I pinned his wrist with my boot before he fired, leaned in close enough he could see the grin that split my face. Then I crushed. His scream broke off wet.

The rest? They ran. Finally. Boots pounding, voices shrill, the name ripping from their throats like a curse.

La Sombra.

They said it louder this time. They screamed it into the night.

And I let them.

Because fear running wild was better than bodies cooling quiet.

I dragged my blade free, flicked blood from it in a red arc across the wall. My pulse was steady now, a drumbeat under the floodlamps. The Presence was gone, shattered, drowned. Nothing between me and the ruin left to make.

And Barceloneta was about to learn what Z's death cost.

The compound gates loomed ahead, metal and chain-link, bristling with rifles. The men on them had heard the screams already. Their radios barked over each other — orders, denials, fear.

And I walked straight at them.

The first volley cracked through the night. Rifles spitting fire, muzzle flashes carving lines across the dark. Bullets hissed past, chipped concrete, snapped steel. One dug into my thigh, another ripped skin from my arm. The rest — noise. Nothing more.

I kept walking.

Their fire faltered first. Men swore, voices rising, the name on their tongues again. *La Sombra.* They tried to reload with hands that shook too much. I was already on the gate.

My fingers locked through chain-link, pulled. Metal screamed, links snapping one by one until the whole section peeled away like wet paper. The men closest stumbled back, rifles useless. I swung the gate sideways, slammed it into three of them. Bone snapped, one skull caved clean under the weight.

The fourth tried to run. I caught his collar, dragged him close, and bit into his throat until the spray painted me red. His body dropped twitching.

Inside, the yard exploded. Floodlights blazed. Men poured out of barracks, pistols and rifles clutched tight. Half of them shouting orders, the other half shouting prayers.

I roared back. A sound too loud for one body, too sharp to be human. It cracked their formation like glass.

They opened fire again, desperate now. Magazines dumped wild. Rounds dug into my chest, tore flesh, carved lines through muscle. I didn't stop. I didn't even flinch. Pain was theirs, not mine.

I hit the first line like a hammer. My fist broke a jaw sideways. My boot crushed a knee backward. I tore a rifle away, swung it like a club, split a man's skull in two strikes.

Another tried to stab me — I caught the blade, twisted it back into his gut, shoved until steel kissed his spine.

The yard filled with screams. Real screams. Not battle shouts. Not orders. Just terror.

More ran. Some fired as they retreated. Others dropped weapons and bolted into the night, shouting the same word into the dark. *La Sombra.*

I didn't chase them. Not yet. I wanted the ones who stood. The ones too slow to break.

I threw a body into the barracks door. The wood splintered, men inside scrambling. I followed, shoulders filling the frame, blade in hand. The first swung at me with a wrench. I split him from collar to hip. His scream cut short, his insides steaming the floor. The others backed away, stumbling over bunks, eyes wide.

I stepped in. Closed the door behind me. And painted the walls red.

When I came back out, the yard was quieter. Fewer rifles. More blood. Bodies stacked, eyes wide, mouths frozen around prayers that hadn't saved them.

But the compound wasn't done. Not yet.

A truck screeched around the corner, lights cutting hard across the yard. Men in the back, rifles braced. They fired wild, the rounds chewing through the air. I ducked low, ripped the nearest corpse up by the collar, and used it for cover. Rounds shredded meat and bone until the body fell apart in my hands.

By then I was already at the truck.

I leapt onto the hood, boots denting steel. The windshield spiderwebbed under the impact. My fist drove through glass, through the driver's skull, until blood fountained over the dash. The truck swerved, slammed into the wall, and the men in the back spilled screaming.

I dragged one up by the ankle, swung him into another. Their heads cracked together, split like melons. A third crawled, begging, whispering to a God who'd already left. I kicked his jaw sideways and kept moving.

The compound stank of blood now. Gunpowder. Smoke. The air was hot with it, thick enough to choke anyone still breathing.

I tore through the hallways next. Door after door. Barracks. Kitchens. Armories. I didn't stop. Didn't slow. Every man I found went into the walls, the floors, the ceilings. Some broke fast. Some begged first. I gave them the same answer. Steel. Bone. Silence.

And always the word followed me. From lips split with fear, from radios choked with static: *La Sombra.*

The deeper I went, the quieter it got. Men stopped shouting. Stopped firing. Stopped standing. Fear worked faster than steel. The compound wasn't holding. It was collapsing.

I walked through it steady. Boots slick, dripping with red. My breath calm, my heart slow. Like this was the rhythm I'd been born for.

And then I heard him.

Marco. His voice, sharp, cutting through the compound chaos. Barking orders, trying to knit his men together with words they no longer believed.

I followed it. Past bodies. Past doors kicked off hinges. Past men who whispered *La Sombra* with their last air before I crushed it out of them.

The hall narrowed, lights buzzing overhead. And at the end, his office. Heavy wood door, steel frame. Guarded by the last line of men too loyal or too afraid to run.

They saw me. Froze. One whispered it again. *La Sombra.*

The others tried to raise rifles. My blade dropped the first before he fired. My fist crushed the second's throat before he screamed. The last two ran, and I let them. Let them carry the word further.

The hall stank of fear and blood. My hand closed on the doorknob.

Marco was inside.

And I was done breaking pawns.

Ghost

Marco

The compound was supposed to feel safe. My fortress. My empire on the water. Concrete thick enough to stop bullets, men thick enough to stop anything else.

But safety cracked when fear took root.

The word spread first. *La Sombra.* I heard it carried through the halls like smoke, starting at the pier and snaking its way inside. Guards who'd stood tall a hundred times suddenly couldn't keep their rifles steady. I smacked one across the mouth for whispering it under his breath, but the look in his eyes stayed.

The look said he believed it.

I stormed back into my office, the bottle on my desk already half gone. My hand shook when I poured, so I gripped the glass tighter until it nearly cracked. The shouts outside bled through the walls—panic where discipline should've been.

"Idiotas," I muttered, pacing hard. "One ghost story and you fall apart."

But the gunfire… the gunfire was wrong. Bursts, short and violent, then nothing. Silence after screams, like someone had cut the air in half. If it had been a raid, the fight would stretch, ebb and flow. This was—clean.

Too clean.

The radio on my desk hissed. A voice cracked through: "Señor—he's—he's in the halls, we can't—" Then a scream, sharp, cut short. The static swallowed it whole.

I slammed my fist down, snarling. "Cowards! All of you!"

But my chest was tight. My throat dry. I took another swallow of rum, let it burn.

A knock at the door. Too fast, too sharp. I snatched my pistol from the desk. "Entra."

One of my lieutenants stumbled in, blood spattered across his shirt that wasn't his. His hands shook when he saluted. "He's tearing through them, Señor. Nothing slows him down."

I stepped close, jammed the muzzle under his chin. "*What* is tearing through them?"

His eyes were wild, whites too big. He whispered it like it was prayer. "La Sombra."

I pulled the trigger. The shot cracked the office, dropped him where he stood. My ears rang, but the silence after rang louder.

The guards outside didn't even flinch. Too afraid to move.

I dragged air in slow, chest tight. "Not a ghost," I muttered. "A man. Just a man."

But the compound said otherwise.

The walls carried every sound now—the boots pounding, the bones breaking, the wet choke of men drowning in their own blood. And under it, always under it, that laugh. Low. Not rushed. Not desperate. A laugh that didn't belong in a place where men died.

I barked orders down the hall, voice raw. "Hold the doors! Hold the line or I'll kill you myself!"

They obeyed. For a minute. Then came the gunfire, and then the screams again. Then silence.

I gripped the desk edge until my knuckles split white.

The radios screamed static, useless. My men stopped answering. The compound that had been a fortress now breathed like a tomb. I paced harder, muttering to myself, cursing them, cursing *him*. My pistol stayed heavy in my hand, but for the first time I felt the weight like it was dragging me under.

Another scream. Close this time. Too close.

Boots scrambled down the hall, pounding toward me. One man rounded the corner, face gray, hands slick with blood that wasn't his. "Señor, he's coming...he's..."

A shadow snapped across the wall behind him. He didn't finish the sentence.

Something pulled him back into the dark like he'd never existed.

Silence again.

I was alone.

The lights flickered once. Twice. Then held steady.

I leveled my pistol at the door, sweat dripping into my eyes. My other hand shook no matter how tight I clenched it.

And then the footsteps came.

Slow. Steady. Like the man owned the hall.

I swallowed hard, barrel trained on the frame, breath ragged.

"La Sombra," I whispered, the word tasting like poison.

And then the door began to open.

The compound was silent. My compound. My kingdom. Silent because every man I owned was bleeding into my floors.

And then the door opened.

He filled the frame like a nightmare I'd never escaped. Blood in his grin, black in his eyes, fists dripping.

My throat burned like it remembered the night he tore it open, left me gurgling on my own blood, crawling while the others escaped. My hand rose there without thinking, fingers pressing scar tissue that never healed right.

"You," I rasped. My voice was gravel, ruined because of him. "Do you even remember me?"

He tilted his head. That grin widened. "No."

White heat cut through my chest. "Of course you don't. I was just another body in your rampage. Another throat you shredded because you couldn't stop. But me?" My nails dug into my scar until blood welled fresh. "I've lived with your hand on my neck every day since. Every word, every bite, every breath, this scar is you."

His eyes didn't blink. Didn't even flicker. "Then I should've pressed harder."

I drew, fired. The bullet split his cheek, spun his head. He laughed as the blood ran down his jaw.

Two steps and I was against the wall, his hand clamped on my throat, the old scar screaming as it ripped again.

"You built an empire out of fear," he said, voice low, shaking the concrete. "Fear I gave you. Tell me Marco, did you ever thank me for it?"

I wheezed against his grip, lips curling bloody. "I didn't just build an empire. I took everything you thought was yours. Even the girl."

His eyes narrowed. Finally, a break in that grin.

"Madison," I hissed, savoring the way the name cut. "She ran to you because she thought you could save her. But I took her back. She's here. In chains. Screaming your name."

The roar that left him cracked the rafters. The lights buzzed, flickered. My feet left the ground, his grip shaking the breath from me. My skull rattled. My ribs screamed.

"You killed Z," he growled, slamming me down so hard the floor split. "Took Madison from me." His fists came down, bone splintering under each blow. "And you think I'll let you live!"

I spat blood onto his face. "She begged when I dragged her back. Just like Z begged before I ended her."

He froze. For a breath. Then the cage around his rage shattered all the way.

He wasn't a man anymore. He was the shadow the whole city whispered about, the one they warned their children of. He was La Sombra.

Fists fell like hammers. My jaw snapped. My ribs caved. Blood filled my mouth until I choked on it. But I forced the laugh, even broken. "She'll die here… and you'll be too late."

He lifted me again, eyes black fire, grin stretched wide and wrong.

"No," he said, voice echoing off the stone. "You die first. And then I tear these walls apart until I find her."

He hurled me into the center of the room, my body breaking against concrete, blood painting the walls.

Blood poured from me in rivers. My jaw hung loose, ribs like shattered glass grinding when I tried to breathe. But I kept laughing, wet and broken, because that was the only weapon I had left.

"You'll tear this place apart," I coughed, spitting red. "But she's already broken. Already mine again."

He didn't answer. Not with words.

His shadow fell over me, blotting out the floodlight overhead. His smile stretched wrong, split with blood and teeth. His eyes weren't eyes — they were void, a place you fell into and never came back.

He bent low, close enough for his breath to scrape my face. "Z's blood is on your hands. Madison's chains are your gift to me. And you think you'll laugh through it?"

His fist came down.

Bone cracked. My vision flashed white.

Another blow. My cheekbone caved, teeth rattling loose.

Another. My skull rang like a bell.

I tried to lift my hands, tried to beg, but his voice drowned me. "Z begged for nothing. Madison begged for freedom. You'll beg for death."

I felt the floor cave under my body as he hammered me down, the concrete itself cracking. Each hit wasn't just flesh and bone—it was vengeance made flesh; fury sharpened to an edge.

I choked on blood, my lungs rattling. "You... you're just... a monster..."

He paused, head tilting like a predator amused with prey. His grin widened. "Exactly."

His hand closed on my throat, the same throat he'd torn open years ago. Scar tissue split under his grip, hot blood spilling fresh. He lifted me off the floor like I weighed nothing, my legs kicking air.

"Remember this?" His voice was thunder in my skull. "I do. Every night I dreamed of finishing it."

He slammed me against the wall, once, twice, the bones in my spine shrieking. My body sagged, limp, but he wasn't done.

His thumbs dug into my neck, fingers curling until I felt everything tear. My vision blurred, then tunneled. His grin was the last thing left.

"You took Z," he whispered. "You chained Madison."

He wrenched hard. Bone snapped. The sound was final.
The world went dark.

(HIM)

I let the corpse fall. Marco's blood smeared my hands, hot
and slick, dripping from my nails. His body hit the cracked
concrete with a hollow thud, his ruined throat spilling what
little voice he had left.

The silence that followed was complete.

Z was gone. Madison was still lost. Nothing I broke would
bring her back. Nothing I killed would free Madison yet.
But Marco was ash, and that was a start.

I stood over him, chest heaving, fists dripping.

"Pawn," I muttered, and turned for the halls.

Because Madison was here. And I wasn't leaving without
her.

Escape

HIM

The compound stank of blood and smoke. My boots left prints across it, slick and dark, like the floor itself couldn't swallow enough. Doors hung crooked, alarms wailed without order. Men didn't guard halls anymore — they cowered in them, praying I'd pass them by.

I didn't.

Their prayers fed me. Their fear fueled me. Every scream carried her name in it, whether they meant it or not.

Z.

The first I found huddled behind a crate, rifle clutched so hard his knuckles split. His finger never touched the trigger. I snapped his neck before he could.

Another ran for the stairwell, boots clattering, voice cracking: *"¡La Sombra! ¡La Sombra!"* The word trailed off when my hand closed on his collar and hurled him into the wall hard enough to paint it red.

I moved like fire eats — wild, directionless, until it finds the fuel it wants most. And the fuel I wanted was at the heart of this place.

The hall turned, and there — Conner.

He staggered out of a doorway, rifle in one hand, his other arm cradling weight too heavy for him. His face was wrecked — swollen, split, the shine of grief in his eyes deeper than the cuts. His shirt was stained dark, and across it lay her.

Z.

Her hair stuck wet to her cheek, her hoodie torn, blood drying in cracks down her skin. Her head lolled against his chest, lips parted but silent.

Conner dropped to his knees when he saw me, not out of reverence, but because his legs finally gave. His breath was ragged, his jaw clenched so hard it shook.

"She's gone," he rasped. His voice broke on it. "They— Marco—"

I didn't let him finish.

I stepped forward, bent low, and took her from his arms. My hands slid under her shoulders, under her knees, lifting her like she weighed nothing. But she weighed everything.

Conner didn't fight me. He just sagged forward, palms pressed to his face like he wanted to claw his own skin off.

I held her close, chest heaving, and the compound itself seemed to hush around us. Men still lived here. I could hear their boots. Hear their panic. But they were already dead.

"Stay on your feet," I said, voice cold, not unkind. "She wouldn't forgive you if you quit here."

Conner lifted his head. His face was ruin, but his eyes still burned. He stood again, rifle gripped, shaking, but ready.

We moved together.

The halls bled enemies into our path, but none lasted. I tore them down with one hand, Z cradled in the other. Throats crushed, skulls shattered, bones splintered. I didn't set her down to kill them. I killed them while holding her, making every death a tithe to her blood.

Conner cleared corners, every shot an answer to the rage I didn't bother to hide. He was a soldier broken open, and I was the shadow that carried him forward.

At last, a door heavier than the rest. Bolted. Reinforced.

I set Z down gently on the floor, brushed a strand of hair from her cheek. For a moment — just one — my hands were soft.

Then I stood and tore the door from its hinges.

Inside.

Madison.

Leather straps and metal chains adorned on her wrists, bruises painting her skin in ugly purple, lip split, one eye swollen. But alive. Awake. Sitting on the cold floor like she'd been waiting for this moment.

Her eyes widened when she saw me. Relief broke first, raw, flooding her face like she'd been holding her breath for days and finally let it out. Then disbelief, like she couldn't trust what she was seeing. Then something deeper, warmer — the kind of love that survives chains and bruises.

Conner shouldered past, his rifle dropping as he rushed to her side. He crouched, voice ragged, "On your feet. I've got you."

She tried. Stumbled. He caught her under the arm, steadying her with the strength he had left.

I lifted Z again, back into my arms, her silence heavier than any chain.

Madison's gaze dropped to the body in my arms. Confusion flickered first — a stranger's face, slack and pale. Her lips parted like she didn't understand why I carried her. Then her eyes cut to Conner, saw the way his shoulders shook, the way his jaw was locked against breaking. The truth hit her then.

Her throat worked, words scraping out. "Oh God… that's your sister."

Conner's silence was answer enough.

Madison's eyes filled, and she turned to each of us in turn, voice breaking. "I'm sorry. I'm so sorry. This is because of me."

I said nothing. Words didn't matter here. Only the weight I carried. Only the blood I still had left to spill.

Conner held Madison upright. I carried Z. Together, we turned from that cell, and the compound trembled under our boots.

Madison kept whispering *I'm sorry* into her palms, her shoulders shaking as Conner half-guided, half-carried her forward. I shifted Z's weight in my arms, the sting of her blood still hot against my chest. Every step through the compound was a grave marker — walls painted with what I'd done, floors slick with what they'd left behind.

The halls narrowed, stinking of cordite and sweat, until a shadow broke the silence ahead. Marco's second. His uniform torn, face streaked with ash, one eye swollen shut. He froze when he saw us, shock cracking into raw hate.

"You," he rasped. His hand twitched toward his weapon.

But Conner was already moving. Rifle slung, fists bare, nothing but grief and rage carrying him forward. He hit the man like a storm, shoulder driving him into the wall. Bone cracked, and the second's breath punched out.

"This is for her," Conner growled, each word a knife. His fists hammered — jaw, ribs, and teeth. The man slid down the wall, dazed, coughing blood. Conner yanked him back up just to slam him down again.

The second spat red, half-smiling through it. "Too late. She's still—"

Conner cut him off with a strike so hard it silenced the breath in his throat. "Shut your mouth."

He didn't stop this time. Not when the man sagged. Not when his knees gave out. Conner's fists kept falling until there was no more sneer left to wipe away. Until the second was nothing but blood and silence at his boots.

Breathing hard, Conner stood over the body, knuckles raw, chest heaving. He spat once, voice like gravel. "Now it's done."

I didn't move. Didn't tell him to stop. This was his kill. His right.

Madison sobbed harder, her voice breaking against her hands.

Conner wiped his face with the back of his wrist, looked at me with eyes that were more hollow than hard. "Let's finish this."

I nodded once, shifted Z higher in my arms. "We walk out together."

And together, bloodied and broken, we pushed through the compound's last shadows.

The compound doors groaned as we shoved them open, the jungle night spilling in thick with damp heat and the stink of salt. My arms burned from Z's weight, but I never loosened my grip. Conner kept Madison close, her face buried against his shoulder, her legs stumbling more than walking. She was alive — bruised, broken, but alive. That was enough for now.

The yard was a graveyard of steel and smoke. The trucks they'd used for patrols sat in crooked lines, doors half-open, bodies slumped against wheels. One still had keys dangling from the ignition, blood on the driver's seat but engine untouched.

"Truck," I said. My voice came out flat, not asking, not offering. Just fact.

Conner guided Madison into the back, laying her against a pile of tarps. I eased Z down beside her, careful, as if laying her on fire would be softer. Madison's eyes caught on Z's face again, wide and wet, confusion breaking into grief all over. I didn't have words to give her. None of us did.

Conner climbed behind the wheel, hands tight on the steering column. I slid into the passenger seat, rifle across my knees, eyes still scanning the compound even though nothing stirred anymore. Everything that could move was already dead.

The engine coughed, sputtered, then caught. Conner jammed it into gear, tires crunching over gravel, rolling us out through gates that no longer had guards to close them. The jungle swallowed us in seconds, dark and wet, the headlights carving tunnels through the green.

No one spoke. Not until the safe house appeared again, shutters closed, generator whining faint in the distance.

Inside, it felt smaller than ever. The map still on the table. The smell of coffee and gun oil still thick. Only now, Z's laptop sat cold, her chair empty.

Conner set Madison down on the cot. She curled into herself, trembling. I laid Z across the table, folding her arms across her chest. My hands lingered too long, knuckles pressed white against her shoulder, before I forced myself back.

Conner broke first. "We can't stay here." His voice was raw, torn from too many fights in too few hours.

He was right. The city would come for us. Marco's death would echo, and Barceloneta wouldn't forgive.

I pulled the sat-phone from Z's bag, flipped it open, thumbed a number I hadn't called in years. Static hummed, then a clipped voice answered.

"Priority extraction," I said. "Barceloneta, Puerto Rico. Airstrip."

The voice didn't argue. Didn't ask questions. Just said: *thirty minutes.*

I snapped the phone shut, shoved it into my pocket. "Pack light. Jet will be there in thirty."

Conner stared at me like he wanted to ask how, who, why, but he didn't. He just nodded, tight, and started pulling what little we had into bags. Madison sat quietly on the cot, watching us with eyes too big, too broken.

I slung a rifle across my back, grabbed the gear I'd stashed, and glanced once more at Z's still form. Then I forced myself toward the door.

"Thirty minutes," I repeated. "We don't miss it."

And together, we carried our dead and our living into the night.

The jungle spat us out onto cracked asphalt, headlights bouncing over weeds that had split the tarmac years ago. The truck rattled hard, engine coughing like it wanted to give out before we made it. But then the airstrip opened ahead — one long scar of concrete under the night.

Floodlights burned at the far end, too clean, too sharp for this forgotten place. And there it was: a jet crouched low, engines humming, silver skin catching the light like a blade. Not cartel, not local. Government. Mine.

Conner's grip tightened on the wheel as we rolled closer. Madison stirred in the back, her head against his shoulder. Z lay across my lap, weight heavier with every mile, every second.

Two men in dark suits stepped out from the glow, no patches, no names. Their rifles hung easy but ready, the kind of easy that came with training. They didn't point them — they didn't have to. They already knew who I was.

One raised a hand, signaling us in. No questions. No delay. Just business.

Conner killed the engine. The silence after felt brutal. For a beat none of us moved. Then he slid out, stiff, ribs bound in bruises. He helped Madison down, her knees buckling until he caught her. She clung to him like he was the last piece of the world holding her up.

I stepped out with Z in my arms. The suits didn't flinch. Didn't ask. One simply opened the hatch, the stairs dropping with a hiss.

Conner looked at me across the hood of the truck. His face was wrecked, hollowed out by grief, by loss. But he nodded once. Not thanks. Not forgiveness. Just... forward.

We climbed. Madison first, leaning hard on Conner. Then me, every step heavier, Z's hair brushing against my sleeve. The cabin was cold, leather seats and humming lights. Too clean for the blood we carried.

The hatch sealed behind us. Engines spooled higher, deep enough to shake the floor.

Through the window, the strip fell away. Barceloneta shrank under us — just another smear of lights in the dark.

Z didn't see it. She never would.

But Madison did. And Conner did. And me, I burned it into memory. Because leaving wasn't escape. Leaving was just the start of what came next.

The Weight We Carry

HIM

The jet hummed low, a different kind of machine than the ones that had haunted Barceloneta. Cleaner. Quieter. No oil stink, no salt rot. Just cold air and the promise of distance.

Z's weight wasn't heavy — it was everything else that was. The silence. The way Conner couldn't look, the way Madison's breath hitched every time a zipper rasped.

I laid her down in the back, stretched her across a couch meant for leather briefcases and soft hands. Someone handed me a body bag; I didn't ask who. My hands moved without me, wrapping her careful, neat, sealing her into black like it made any difference.

She looked smaller like that. Too small. Z had always filled space bigger than she was. Now the jet had her quiet, and I hated it.

When I came back forward, Conner still sat with his head in his hands, rifle propped against his knee like it was the only thing keeping him upright. Madison leaned sideways in her seat, bruised and shaking, but alive. Her eyes tracked me as I sat. She didn't say anything. Just leaned into me, cheek against my arm, like she thought if she let go I'd vanish too.

I didn't lean back. Couldn't. My head was already somewhere else.

London.

She'd hated the rain. Always said it made the streets smell like rot and old newspapers. But she'd walk with me anyway, hood up, hands in her pockets, rambling about code and firewalls while I pretended I wasn't listening. She'd catch me smiling, shove my shoulder, call me a creep for eavesdropping on her genius.

On one specific night, that first night, her head had been bent over blueprints then, not digital but paper, spread across a café table that stank of burnt espresso. London rain hammered the glass, drowning the streets, but she didn't look up. She tapped her pen like a metronome, mouth running about signal towers, choke points, networks the government swore were invisible.

I'd been half-dead, running on nothing but instinct and the scraps of a mission. But she saw me. Really saw me. Didn't care about the blood under my nails, the haunted way I kept scanning doors. She told me to sit, shoved a mug at me, called me a bastard when I didn't drink it fast enough.

That was Z. She never asked permission to save someone.

On rooftops she was louder, braver. Wires in her teeth, laughter sharp enough to cut the dark. She'd tell me about London's veins, how the whole city pulsed with signals nobody understood but her. She said she could hear it, the hum behind the hum. I told her she was insane. She told me I was boring. And then she'd prove herself right, over and over, until I stopped arguing.

She'd been fire when I was nothing but ash. And I hadn't realized until now how much I'd needed her.

The jet hummed, steady. Too steady. My mind dragged me back to that night in the East End, when she pulled me off a floor slick with blood. I'd been gone. ME, not Michael, not Jace, not Lucian, but ME, tearing everything apart. And she didn't run. Didn't scream. She grabbed my face with hands that smelled like solder and sweat and told me I was still there. That I hadn't drowned. That I could still come back.

No one else had ever dared.

Other nights we had endless talks on rooftops, her tapping wires into radios while I kept watch. She'd talk about wanting something bigger, something louder, like the world would finally hear her if she just screamed right. I'd tell her she was already too loud. She'd flip me off, grin like sin, and keep talking.

Countless moments stitched into me like scars. And all of them ended in this. Black bag, cold couch, the jet humming her into silence.

Madison shifted closer. I could feel her breath on my sleeve, her body shaking with more than cold. I didn't move. Couldn't. My hands were still wrapped around Z in my head, carrying her up, laying her down, sealing her away.

The weight wasn't her body. It was every piece of me she'd built, every laugh, every fight, every fire. And now I had to carry all of it alone.

Madison's weight leaned harder into me. I let her. My arm twitched, almost moving around her shoulders, but it fell back still. My head was too loud, too full of Z's voice — calling me boring, calling me reckless, calling me needed.

I closed my eyes. Saw her on that café table, pen tapping, grin sharp. Saw her rooftop laughter under storm clouds. Saw her hands pulling me out of blood and shadow.

The jet's hum filled the silence we couldn't. Conner hadn't moved. His shoulders were stone, but stone cracks, I could hear it in the way his breath caught, in the way his knee bounced against the rifle. He'd lost blood, bruises dark across his cheek and ribs, but none of that touched what broke him now. His sister zipped away behind us.

I wanted to tell him something. Anything. But what was left to say? Words don't mean shit when the body is still warm.

Madison trembled against me. Not from fear, not entirely. She'd lived fear long enough that it was another layer of skin. This was different. Loss without knowing the weight of it. She'd only just learned Z's face before it was taken. The apology in her eyes still burned. As if she thought saying "I'm sorry" to ghosts would change the ledger.

I didn't tell her it wouldn't. I didn't tell her that guilt never left, that it carved itself into you until you thought in its voice. Because that was a truth she already knew.

The hum blurred into memory again. A rooftop in Whitechapel, Z crouched with pliers between her teeth, muttering curses at a junction box. Rain dripping off her hood. She'd spat the pliers into her hand and snapped, "Cover me, asshole, unless you *want* a bullet in my back." I'd covered her. Always.

I opened my eyes. The jet's walls pressed in — white leather, polished chrome, sterile. Nothing of her belonged here. Z had lived in static and neon, in cigarette smoke and wires, in chaos she bent into signal. This coffin of quiet felt wrong for her. Too neat. Too calm.

"She'd hate this," I muttered before I could stop myself.

Madison lifted her head slightly. "What?"

"This," I said, sweeping a hand at the polished cabin. "Silent ride. Clean leather. Easy flight home. She'd want noise. Sparks. To feel like she was still burning even after."

Madison didn't answer. Maybe she didn't know how. Maybe there was no answer. She leaned back in, pressing her forehead against my arm, as if she thought she could anchor me there.

But anchors don't hold when the sea itself is broken.

The bag sat at the back of the jet. I didn't need to see it. I carried it with me already.

The weight we carried wasn't the body. It was the silence that followed.

Conner finally moved. Just one sound at first — a laugh that wasn't a laugh. Hollow. Bitter. It cracked through the cabin louder than the jet itself.

I turned my head, slow. He hadn't lifted his face from his hands. When he finally did, his eyes were bloodshot, rimmed red, the kind of stare that could cut a man in half if it meant getting an answer.

"You were supposed to keep her alive." His voice was gravel. No accusation at first. Just a fact he couldn't spit out without breaking.

I didn't flinch. "We all were."

He barked out something sharp — could've been a laugh, could've been a sob. "Don't give me that. You. All of you. Michael with his plans. Jace with his timing. Lucian with his bullshit tongue. You had every angle covered, didn't you? And still she's back there zipped in black while we sit breathing."

Madison's hand tightened on my sleeve. I didn't move.

"She knew the risks," I said finally. Quiet. Steady. "She chose to step into the fire same as us."

"She wasn't supposed to *die for us*," Conner snapped, voice cracking open now. He shoved his rifle upright, grip white-knuckled like he wanted to use it. "She wasn't supposed to buy our seconds with her last breath."

I leaned forward, elbows on my knees, eyes on his. Cold. Sharp. "She made that choice. Not me. Not you. She knew exactly what it meant when she ran out there."

His jaw worked like he was grinding teeth to dust. "Then what the fuck was the point of you?"

The silence hit harder than his words. Madison flinched. The hum seemed to stop.

I didn't answer right away. Just let it sit there, let it cut. When I finally spoke, my voice was lower than before, the kind of tone that carved instead of shouted.

"The point was that Z trusted me enough to step out there knowing I'd finish it. That's what I did. Marco's gone. His second's gone. His men are ash. And she—" My throat tightened, but I forced the words. "She doesn't have to carry it anymore. That's on me now."

Conner shook his head, breath stuttering. "You think that makes it better?"

"No." I leaned back, eyes never leaving his. "It just makes it done."

The hum pressed back in. Madison shifted against me, her body trembling again. Conner broke first, dragging both hands down his face like he could scrape the grief off with his nails.

He dragged a breath in, long and ragged, then leaned back in his seat. The rifle stayed across his knees, his fingers twitching once before they finally stilled. The edge in him dulled — not gone, never gone, but dulled enough that the words came out quieter.

"...You know," he muttered, eyes fixed on the floor, "I never actually asked."

I frowned. "Asked what?"

He looked up at me then, really looked. Past the blood still drying on my collar, past Madison clinging to my arm, past the weight of Z zipped black behind us. His stare was searching. Cutting.

"Who the hell are you? Really." His jaw flexed once. "Not Michael. Not Jace. Not that smooth bastard Lucian. You."

The question hung there like smoke. Madison turned her face up toward me too, eyes swollen but waiting.

For a long moment, I said nothing. The jet hummed steady, Z's silence sitting heavier than the engines.

Then I leaned back, slow, gaze dropping to my own hands, scarred, cracked, still trembling from the storm I'd unleashed.

"I'm the one they don't talk about," I said finally, voice low. "The one they keep locked in the dark until the world is already burning. I'm what's left when the plans break, when timing fails, when charm dies in the dirt."

I lifted my eyes to his, steady now. Cold. Certain.

"I'm HIM."

Conner's brow furrowed, confusion flickering into something sharper. He sat with it, tested the name on his tongue without speaking it out loud. Then he nodded once — curt, final.

"Figures," he said, voice rough. "You feel like the kind of bastard that only shows up when everything's already gone to hell."

I didn't smile. Didn't need to. "That's because I am."

Conner didn't look away after I said it. He sat there, rifle across his knees, eyes narrowed like he was still weighing whether to spit or nod. Finally, his voice came, rough as gravel.

"So… walk me through it. All of it. 'Cause I've been sitting here pretending I understand, and I don't."

I leaned forward, elbows on my knees, hands loose between them. "You already know the names. Michael. Jace. Lucian." I tapped my temple. "They're pieces. Fragments carved out over years. Michael plans, Jace moves, Lucian talks. They trade the wheel depending on what's needed."

"And you?" Conner asked, eyes narrowing.

I met his stare. "I'm the storm they keep chained up. The violence. The part of him that doesn't stop once the blood starts. I only come out when the cage breaks, or when…" My jaw tightened. "…when grief tears the locks off."

Madison flinched faintly at that. She didn't need me to say Z's name. It was already heavy enough in the air.

Conner dragged a hand down his face, exhaling like he was trying to process a language he'd never learned. "So when I look at you — I'm looking at all of them, or just one?"

"Both," I said. "One body, one life. Four edges. You'll always see the same face, but if you're paying attention…" My eyes narrowed, voice low. "You'll know who's steering."

Silence stretched again, but it wasn't the same silence from before. Not sharp. Not hostile. Just heavy. Like the words had weight enough on their own.

The jet dipped, banking low. The pilot's voice cracked over comms: "New York in sight. Fifteen minutes."

Madison straightened, clutching her seat belt like she could hold the world still. Conner leaned back, head hitting the wall, rifle still across his knees. I sat between them, the hum of the engines running steady under our silence.

We landed smooth. Wheels biting tarmac, engines whining down. The hatch hissed open to cold night air that tasted cleaner than it had any right to. Home. Or something pretending to be it.

The ride back was quiet. No words left worth spilling. When we finally climbed the stairs into the apartment, the air hit with the familiar sting of dust and old coffee. Lights too dim, silence too loud. Safe, but not whole. Never whole again.

I dropped into a chair, running a hand over my face. Conner leaned his rifle against the wall, collapsed into the couch. Madison perched at the edge, still shaking, but breathing. Alive.

And then it hit me. Sharp. Sudden.

"Shit." I stood, jaw tight, moving toward the bedroom door.

Conner blinked. "What?"

I didn't look back. "The others. Michael. Jace. Lucian. When I come out, when I stay out too long…" My throat tightened. "…sometimes I hurt them. Pressure, cracks. They carry the weight whether they want to or not. I need to check on them."

The room fell silent again. Madison's eyes followed me, wide. Conner just sat there, lips pressed thin, saying nothing.

I put my hand on the door, the hum of the plane still in my bones, Z's laughter still echoing in my head. And I knew, whatever waited behind that door wasn't going to be easy.

But I had to face it.

Repercussion

Mindscape

The apartment was too quiet. Even New York's endless noise felt distant, muffled through the glass, like the city itself didn't want to intrude. Conner and Madison were in the other room, their voices low, too tired to rise above the hum of the radiator. I didn't join them. Couldn't.

Instead, I made for the bedroom. Boots heavy, chest tight, the kind of heaviness you can't shake no matter how many times you roll your shoulders. The bed sat unmade, sheets tangled from nights when no one really slept. I sat down slow, the springs groaning under me, then let myself fall back, shoulders sinking into the mattress, eyes tracing the cracked plaster in the ceiling.

The hum was already there, crawling in my skull, that ever-present static of them. The others. All I had to do was close my eyes and the static turned into doors.

So I did.

The mindscape surged open. A place of shadows and echoes, the table in the center where we always gathered. Except it didn't look right this time. It was splintered, edges blackened, like someone had set fire to it and walked away before the flames went out. Smoke clung to the air. The walls, if you could call them that, shuddered, pulsing like something broken trying to hold itself together.

Michael was already there. Standing, rigid, fists tight at his sides, eyes locked on me like I was a target he'd been waiting years to put down. Lucian lounged in a chair, the picture of lazy defiance, but even his grin was wrong, thin, brittle, a knife's edge without polish.

I raised my hands, slow, palms open. You can take the wheel. Any of you. If you want it, it's yours.

The words echoed in the smoke, heavier than I meant them to be. I expected questions, a storm of them. Where had I been? Why hadn't I fought harder? Why did it take Z's death to tear me free? I braced for it.

But Michael didn't ask.

He moved. Fast.

His fist cracked across my jaw before I even thought to block. Pain lit the side of my skull, sharp and real, too real for something born inside the mind. My head snapped sideways, teeth grinding. Blood tasted like metal in my mouth.

Michael's voice shook the ground. What did you do?

I blinked, spat red into the dark. I—

Another blow. Harder. My ribs this time, the kind of punch meant to shatter. I staggered, breath tearing out of me.

What did you do?! *he roared again, louder, raw, eyes burning with something hotter than rage.*

The table trembled. Lucian didn't move to stop him. Didn't smile. Just leaned forward, watching with eyes that were too sharp, too knowing. Like he already had the answer and wanted me to choke on it myself.

I forced myself upright, clutching my side, voice hoarse. I offered you the wheel. I'm giving it back—

Michael grabbed my collar, dragged me close, teeth bared. We don't want your scraps. We want the truth. Where the hell is he?

The smoke pressed heavier, the black edges creeping closer. I could feel it before I could say it, the gap, the absence that gnawed where someone should've been. The air was too empty.

I froze. Looked past Michael. Looked to the table.

One chair was missing.

Lucian's voice slid out, low, dangerous. Tell him, Michael.

Michael's grip tightened, knuckles white, eyes still burning holes through me. You want to give us something? Give us him.

The air snapped tight in my chest. Because for the first time since the cage broke, I realized it wasn't just the table that had burned. It was the seat Jace should've been sitting in.

Michael's grip was iron, his eyes inches from mine, fury bright enough to scorch. His knuckles dug into my collarbone, holding me in place like he could break me with nothing but his will.

Give us him, *he growled again, every word low, dangerous.*

I shook my head hard, jaw clenched. He's here. He has to be here.

Michael's fist came again, cracking against my cheek, snapping my head sideways. Pain lit white behind my eyes, ringing in my skull. I staggered but didn't fall.

He's not, *Michael barked, voice raw.* Open your eyes! Look at the table!

I turned, vision swimming, searching for him. That stupid straight-backed posture, the way he never leaned because discipline was always in his spine. The voice that timed everything, that pulled me out of rage by counting doors and clocks. Jace should've been there.

But the seat was empty.

No, *I hissed, shaking my head, teeth grinding.* He's hiding. He does that when he's tired. He's... he's here.

Michael slammed me against the table, the splintered wood biting into my back. His face twisted with rage and grief. He's gone. You ripped him out!

My hands locked around his wrists, nails biting into his skin, but I couldn't shove him off. Couldn't make myself strike back. My throat felt raw, words shredding out. I didn't—I wouldn't—

Lucian finally moved. Slow. Deliberate. He leaned forward out of the shadows, elbows on his knees, grin gone, eyes dark.

You did, *Lucian said softly.* You tore the wheel out of Michael's hands when Z died. Jace sensed you and tried to hold you back. You dragged it so hard you snapped something. And now? *He flicked two fingers at the empty chair.* Now there's nothing left to sit there.

The smoke thickened, the broken table groaned under me, and the truth pressed in sharp as glass. The absence wasn't just silence. It was hollow. It was void.

No... *My voice cracked.* He's still—

Michael's fist slammed into the table inches from my head, splinters flying. He roared it in my face: WHAT DID YOU DO?

The whole mindscape shook with the sound, walls bowing inward, black smoke spilling through the cracks. I felt my own chest cave under it, breath rattling, rage choking me.

But I forced the words out, even as my voice broke: I just wanted to protect you. All of you. I didn't mean to—

Lucian's laugh was cold, humorless. Intent doesn't matter, brother. Result does. And the result? *He leaned closer, voice cutting like a blade.* Boy Scout's gone.

The words cut deeper than Michael's fists ever could. The empty chair glared back at me, louder than any scream. And for the first time, I couldn't convince myself otherwise.

Jace. Was. Gone.

Vengeance

The jet cut through gray dawn like a blade, its engines low and steady, too calm for the storm waiting below. Barceloneta's strip of cracked asphalt stretched narrow beneath us, the jungle pressing on all sides, the sea gnawing close on the edges. This was no place for a landing, but it had always been enough for us. For me.

The wheels screamed when they met the ground, rubber tearing across pavement that had been patched too many times. The fuselage shuddered once before settling, smooth again, as though nothing could shake its bones.

I rose before the jet even stopped moving. My men followed suit without hesitation. Twelve of them, dressed in pressed black despite the humidity, rifles held with discipline the rest of the world forgot existed. They were not boys. They were not thugs. They were my shadows, the last line of flesh between me and a world that had been trying to erase me for forty years.

The jet slowed, nose dipping, the tires groaning. Before the stairs were even fully extended, I stepped down, polished shoes meeting the tarmac with a deliberate click.

The heat hit instantly. Heavy. Humid. Salt and smoke fused in the air, clinging to the skin like a second layer. I did not flinch. I adjusted my cufflinks instead — platinum, not gold. Subtle, but final.

The jungle hissed around us, alive with insects and distant birds, but here, closer to the compound, the silence pressed wrong. Too deep.

I lifted my chin, breathing in slow. No sound of guards on rotation. No chatter of radios. No laughter of the younger recruits who always smoked too close to the fence.

Silence meant only one thing.

Death.

One of the captains shifted close, his voice low, wary. "Señor… it's too quiet."

I didn't look at him. My eyes stayed locked on the compound walls visible beyond the gate, their tops jagged with rusted barbed wire. "Quiet is not safety," I said. My voice did not rise. It never had to. "Quiet means the noise is already finished."

We walked, my shadows fanning out wide as we crossed the tarmac toward the yawning steel gates. The sun hadn't fully climbed, but the floodlamps mounted along the walls still buzzed, casting pale cones across the ground. They lit more than they were meant to.

Bullet holes. Chewed steel. Black scars across the gates like claw marks from a beast.

The hinges hung crooked, the gates half-open as though they had given up.

My shoes crunched over something brittle. A shell casing bent and bloodied. Then another. And another.

I did not slow.

My men hesitated at the threshold, rifles up, eyes cutting every angle, but I did not break stride.

When death waits inside, you do not pause at the door.

You walk in.

The compound greeted me with silence. Not the stillness of order — but the silence of something ended.

My shoes pressed into dirt gone tacky with blood. It had dried in streaks down the concrete, pooled under the gates, soaked into the dust. My men shifted behind me, boots crunching on spent shells, the faint metallic rattle of rifles too loud in this place.

Bodies slumped along the walls like discarded uniforms. Their coveralls were torn; faces twisted in the last panic before the end. My men looked down at them with the eyes of soldiers, cataloguing wounds, patterns, numbers. But me?

I looked at the hands.

Hands tell more than faces. And these hands were raw, split, torn by grips too desperate. Some clutched their rifles even in death. Others reached for wounds that bled too long. But all of them had failed. My men. My blood. My house.

One of my captains broke the hush, voice tight. "Señor, there are… too many."

"Count," I said.

He dropped to a knee instantly, gesturing for others to begin tallying. I did not need numbers, but order is built on ritual, and rituals must be obeyed.

I walked deeper, the gates sagging behind me.

The walls loomed higher inside, but they felt smaller now. Compounds are supposed to breathe fear. Supposed to press down on intruders until their courage cracks.

But what happens when the walls cannot contain the monster?

I knew the answer. I'd built these walls myself.

The first courtyard stretched wide, its concrete cracked from years of weight. Now it was broken in other ways. Bullet trails clawed across the far wall. The air reeked of cordite, sweat, and something heavier — iron, copper, the stink of blood spilled too fast for earth to drink.

Boots dragged behind me. "Señor," another man said. He pointed.

The courtyard fountain, once a useless ornament I had mocked my son for keeping, was choked red. Bodies floated in water too shallow to hold them, faces glassy, arms tangled like weeds.

I felt the heat press heavier, sweat threatening my brow, but I did not raise a hand. A man like me never wipes his forehead.

Instead, I stood at the fountain and let my men gather, rifles steady, eyes darting. "Who did this?" one of them whispered, though not to me. Fear made them speak like children.

I answered anyway.

"Not who," I said. My voice was calm. Always calm. "What."

The word hung in the courtyard, heavier than the smell.

Because this was not work done by Marco's rivals. Not by the police. Not by rebels.

This was something else. Something that had torn through trained men like paper, that had left silence where noise should have ruled.

I turned from the fountain and kept walking.

The fountain was behind me, but its stink clung to my nose. I stepped into the main hall, the echo of my shoes hollow against concrete that had once carried the weight of Marco's ambitions.

The air was different here. Close. Heavy. The kind of silence that doesn't just exist, it waits.

My men followed, rifles raised, though what good were rifles against something that could do *this*?

Blood painted the walls in arcs too wide to be bullets. The trail of a man dragged screaming. Another slammed so hard into plaster his outline still remained, a grotesque shadow burned in dust and red.

I stopped at the first doorway. The office had once belonged to one of Marco's lieutenants. Inside, the desk was split clean down the middle. The man himself hung over the jagged edge, throat torn so deep I could see spine. His eyes bulged, his mouth frozen mid-prayer.

One of my captains muttered, "Dios…"

"Quiet," I snapped. My voice did not rise, but it cracked like a whip in the dark. He bit his tongue bloody and lowered his head.

I moved on.

Every door I passed told another story. A guard with his jaw shattered sideways, teeth scattered across tile. Another slumped against the wall, chest caved in where something stronger than a man had hit him. Their rifles lay discarded, bent, useless.

Bent. Like toys.

The deeper we walked, the clearer it became: this was not a battle. This was punishment. A message carved in bodies and silence.

Marco had been foolish enough to think his compound was fortress. Walls, men, weapons — all meaningless.

I paused again, my eyes falling on a trail smeared across the floor. It dragged into the infirmary.

Inside, beds had been overturned, sheets ripped, drawers emptied. And at the far wall, scrawled with bloody fingers, one word glared back at me.

Sombra.

The men behind me murmured, uneasy. The word was older than most of them. A story told in whispers. Mothers used it to scare children from wandering the alleys after dark.

But here, it was not a story. Here, it was proof.

"La Sombra," one finally said, too loud.

I turned on him so fast he flinched. "Shut your mouth."

His lips trembled shut, but I saw the fear in his eyes. He believed it. They all did.

And maybe they were right.

I straightened, smoothing the front of my suit with slow precision. Fear is for children. Men like me shape fear into a weapon.

But even I could not look at these walls, these bodies, and pretend it was just a man.

This was wrath. Pure. Unleashed.

And if wrath had a name, it wasn't mine. It wasn't Marco's. It was something older. Something darker.

I walked on.

The hallways bled into the great chamber. Marco had always called it his *office*, but I knew better. He thought of it as a throne room — the center of his empire, the place where men crawled on their knees to pledge loyalty, where women were paraded like jewels.

The heavy doors hung crooked now, one hinge snapped. A smear of red handprints marked the wood where someone had tried to claw their way out.

I stepped inside.

The first thing that hit me was the smell. Not blood, not gunpowder — though there was plenty of both. It was rot. Something deeper. The scent of pride gutted.

Marco's chair — his throne — lay toppled on its side. The rug was soaked, dark with pooled blood that had crept into every stitch. Papers were scattered like leaves after a storm.

And at the far end of the room, slumped against the wall, was my son.

Marco.

His eyes were still open, glassy, fixed on the ceiling like he couldn't believe he was staring at it from the floor. His throat... Dios, his throat. Ripped apart, ragged, half-healed scar tissue shredded fresh again. I knew that wound. I *remembered* the first time it was carved into him — years ago, by the same shadow that had haunted us tonight.

"La Sombra," one of my men whispered behind me.

The name tasted like ash in my mouth. The shadow my son had mocked, dismissed, called a story for cowards — it had returned to finish what it started.

I walked closer, each step deliberate. My shoes sank into the rug, sticky with what was left of him.

Marco's hand was curled around his pistol, empty. His other hand clawed at his chest, as though even at the end he still thought himself strong enough to fight.

I crouched, slow, my knees groaning with the weight of age and fury. My fingers brushed his hair back, the way I had when he was a boy, before the cartel, before the empire. His skin was cold.

"You stupid child," I whispered. My voice didn't tremble, though everything inside me wanted to. "I told you a woman would be your downfall. And it was. I see it now."

The silence swallowed me, the room pressing in tight.

"You had everything. Men. Power. Fear. And you squandered it." My thumb dragged across the torn edge of his throat. "He came back for you. The shadow you mocked. The man who marked you all those years ago. And now you're dust because you never learned to listen."

I stood again, straightened my suit jacket, and let the coldness settle in me like steel.

My son was gone. His empire burned. His men broken.

But I was not gone.

I turned, my voice steady, clear, slicing through the chamber like a blade.

"Clean this place. Burn the dead. What remains is mine now."

My men hesitated. They looked at Marco, then at me, and I saw the flicker in their eyes — the shift. He was gone. I was not. Loyalty moves fast when survival demands it.

I looked back at Marco's body one last time. My jaw locked. My chest did not heave. Grief had no place here. Only vengeance.

"Find him," I said, my voice low, dangerous. "Find *La Sombra*. Find the ones who walked with him. I don't care what it takes."

The men nodded. Fear made them eager.

I stepped over my son's corpse and walked back into the hall, the ruin of his empire groaning in silence around me.

The hunt had already begun.

The courtyard opened before me like the carcass of a slaughtered bull. Floodlamps buzzed overhead, throwing their pale light across bodies stacked where they'd fallen. Guards, lieutenants, errand boys — men who thought the compound walls made them untouchable.

Not tonight.

The ground was slick with rain and blood, puddles spreading crimson in the cracks of the stone. Trucks burned in crooked rows, their skeletons glowing faintly, the smell of diesel thick enough to coat the lungs.

I stepped into it without flinching. My shoes soaked, my suit catching the stink of smoke, but I didn't care.

Men followed, careful, their boots crunching glass and bone. They whispered among themselves, voices sharp with fear. I didn't need to hear the words. They only knew one name now, La Sombra.

I stopped in the center of it all. Bodies ringed me, arms twisted, eyes open, mouths frozen mid-scream. And I looked up, past the floodlamps, into the night sky.

It was clear. Stars stretched wide, clean, endless. A cruel contrast to the ruin below.

I let the silence hang until even the whispers behind me died. Then I spoke.

"This," I said, my voice carrying over the blood-soaked stones, "is the measure of my son's weakness."

No one answered. None dared.

"He let himself be haunted. He let a ghost undo what generations built. And now…" I swept a hand across the ruin. "Now I inherit ash."

A pause. I let the weight settle, let them feel the gravity of my calm.

"But understand me. Ash is not an ending. It is what fire leaves behind before something greater rises."

I turned, slowly, letting my gaze pierce through the men who'd followed me out here. Some wouldn't meet my eyes. Others straightened, desperate to show they still belonged.

"I will not weep for him," I said. "I will not forgive him. I will not forgive *her*—the woman who made him weak. Or the shadow who came back to finish him."

I took a breath, slow, steady, the stars still cold above.

"This is not over. This is the beginning."

My voice hardened, iron drawn from grief.

"I want names. I want routes. I want whispers dragged out of every rat in this city. I want the shadow hunted until the world itself forgets the stars and remembers only my wrath."

A murmur rippled through the men. Fear, yes. But loyalty too — loyalty carved from terror.

I looked once more at the carnage, the proof of La Sombra's return, and let my voice drop to a whisper that carried like a blade.

"They think they've killed a son. But what they've done is awaken a father."

The courtyard stayed silent, save for the hiss of burning trucks. And in that silence, vengeance rooted itself like stone.

I didn't stay there long; I had calls to make.

The war room smelled of damp concrete and blood. Generators sputtered in the corner, struggling to power the few working lights. Half the screens were dead, cables ripped out, sparks still blackening the walls.

I walked in slow, letting the men already gathered hear the weight of my steps. They rose from their chairs like schoolboys caught cheating. Not one met my eye.

The table in the center was still smeared with blood — not Marco's, not yet, but one of his captains. His body had been dragged aside, leaving the red stain behind like a signature.

I placed my hands on that stain. Pressed down until my palms felt sticky. Then I looked at them.

"Call the others," I said flatly.

Phones came out. Scrambling. One man cursed when his signal failed, fumbling for the backup satellite rig. Another stammered about the council being scattered. I silenced them with a glance.

Minutes later, the screen lit. One by one, faces filled it. Older men, younger lieutenants, some bloated with money, others lean with hunger. All cartel. All mine now.

They greeted me with caution, not respect. They knew why I was calling.

"My son is dead," I told them. No softening. No excuses. "Marco is gone."

Murmurs. Crossed faces. Some feigned sorrow. Others smirked, already tasting the shift in power.

I cut through them all. "Don't waste breath. His failure was mine to bury, and I have buried it. But understand me now: his killer is no man. No soldier. He is the shadow you whisper to your children to keep them inside at night."

One of the younger ones scoffed. "A myth, viejo."

I leaned closer to the screen, my voice a blade. "I have walked the halls where he left his mark. I have stepped through the blood of my son's men. I have seen the fear in the eyes of those who survived. It is not a myth. It is real. And it has chosen war with us."

Silence spread across the screen. The word was already in their heads — La Sombra.

I nodded once. "So we give him war. Every port. Every street. Every whisper of his presence, I want it fed back here. We choke him with numbers. We drown him with fire. And we do not stop until the world itself knows the cartel is not afraid of shadows."

The older faces nodded. Reluctant, but nodding all the same. One or two muttered about the cost, about lost shipments, about timing. I didn't let them finish.

"The cost," I said coldly, "is nothing compared to weakness. And I will not watch weakness spread through this family like a rot."

The silence that followed was obedience. The kind born of terror.

I drew a cigar from my pocket, lit it off the generator's hiss of flame, and blew smoke into the blood-stained air.

"They think they've won," I said, voice low but cutting through the screen. "But we do not end. We multiply. We sharpen. We become more than they can ever bury."

One last drag. One last exhale.

"This is not revenge. This is reclamation. And it begins tonight."

The screen went black, the council dismissed. Only the hum of the dying generator and the reek of smoke remained.

I stood alone in the ruin of my son's empire, already imagining how much larger mine would grow once the shadow was bled dry.

They left the room when I told them to.
No arguments. No hesitation. They knew better.

The door shut behind them, leaving me with the silence of the compound's morgue. A steel table, a buzzing light, and the shape of my son under a sheet.

I didn't move at first. Just stood there, cigar burning down between my fingers, smoke curling lazy toward the ceiling. The same ceiling Marco had once run through as a boy, climbing beams he had no business on, laughing too loud, daring me to catch him.

I set the cigar down on the tray. Pulled the sheet back.

His face was pale, jaw slack, throat carved with an old scar I remembered too well — the scar left by HIM, years ago, when I should have crushed the monster before he ever had the chance to rise again.

And now Marco was gone.

I pressed my hand against the cold of his chest. Not out of tenderness. Not grief. Just to feel the finality of it.

"You were reckless," I said quietly. My voice echoed against the steel walls. "Too much pride. Too little patience. And now look at you."

For a moment, I let myself feel it — the anger, the loss, the weight. Then I crushed it down, because weight was weakness, and weakness had no place here.

"I told you once," I murmured, brushing the scar on his throat with my thumb, "that a woman would be your downfall. And I was right."

The air hummed heavier.

"But his hand delivered the blow. That shadow. That ghost. La Sombra."

I leaned close, close enough my words would've filled his ear if he could still hear. "I will find him. And when I do, I will not bury him. I will erase him. Piece by piece. I will salt the ground he walks on, break the bodies he hides behind, burn every memory of him from this earth until not even the grave remembers his name."

My hand curled into a fist against Marco's chest.

"This is my vow to you, hijo."

I pulled the sheet back up, covering his face, sealing him into silence. Then I stood straight, shoulders squared, eyes burning cold enough to freeze the room itself.

I turned for the door. Not once did I look back.

Because vengeance didn't wait.

And my son's shadow would not die quietly.

The Presence

I've got to let them continue to think he's gone. It's the only way this will work. I can't keep going like this. Year after year.

It's been over a decade, watching from the inside out. None of them noticing me. Hell, I didn't notice myself till I was about eighteen.

First it was Jace, the watcher I called him, then came Michael. True to the title they've all given him, the strategist. He was created cause Jace felt too alone. For a couple of years, it was just them. Then Lucian was born, created, manifested? Who cares, he was there for one purpose. Yeah, you know what that is, you don't need me to explain it.

Then HIM was there. Created after Jace got so low he thought the only way out was a bullet. How HIM managed to take control at the last second and move the gun just a few inches is still beyond my comprehension.

But me, I'm what came before Jace. I'm the original, I am all of them and none of them. I've been here, in the darkness, waiting, trying to reach out to them. Protecting them when even HIM fails.

I tried teaching HIM, that he isn't always needed but look where that got me. I had to run and get Jace out the way before he was bulldozed over. That reckless oaf.

I've carried this too long. Longer than they'll ever know. They think their fragments and pieces cracked off from something else. They don't understand that all of them came from me. Jace, Michael, Lucian, HIM... all just reflections when the mirror shattered.

And I let them think I was nothing. A cage. A shadow. But I was here first. Before the scars. Before the blood. Before the bullet that almost ended it. I was the boy who opened his eyes in a world too sharp and too cruel. I was the one who broke.

My name…

It feels strange to drag it up again, like pulling a stone out of the deepest part of the river. But it's mine. It was always mine.

Asher Marks.

And this is my story.

Author's Thank You

To my editor and friend, Brittany. Thank you for always being there. For the late-night calls when I couldn't shut up about some wild idea. For letting me yammer until it all came out right. For reminding me, over and over again, to stay true to the story when I started to drift. You've been more than an editor through this, you've been a friend who believed in me when I didn't believe in myself.

And to my readers, you don't know how much it means that you're still here. That you chose to keep walking with me, even when the path gets darker and heavier. I don't take that lightly. Your time, your belief, your willingness to dive into this world with me—it means everything.

I may write in shadows, but I don't walk them alone. Thanks to Brittany. Thanks to you. I wouldn't be here without you, and I sure as hell wouldn't keep going without you either.